WILD COUNTRY

**Center Point
Large Print**

**This Large Print Book carries the
Seal of Approval of N.A.V.H.**

WILD COUNTRY

Noel M. Loomis

CENTER POINT PUBLISHING
THORNDIKE, MAINE

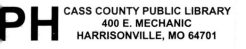

This Center Point Large Print edition
is published in the year 2008 by arrangement with
Golden West Literary Agency.

The text of this Large Print edition is unabridged. In other
aspects, this book may vary from the original edition.
Printed in the United States of America.
Set in 16-point Times New Roman type.

ISBN: 978-1-60285-285-3

Library of Congress Cataloging-in-Publication Data

Loomis, Noel M., 1905-1969.
    Wild country / Noel M. Loomis.--Center Point large print ed.
        p. cm.
    ISBN: 978-1-60285-285-3 (lib. bdg. : alk. paper)
        1. Large type books. I. Title.

PS3523.O554W55 2008
813'.54--dc22

2008018059

A Salute to
THE WESTERN WRITERS OF AMERICA
an association of writers who are proud of their
heritage and who try to be worthy of it. Some day
America will be proud of them.

WILD COUNTRY

1 ROGER ADAMS had heard about Hughes' Groggery. What he had heard wasn't good, but he planned to go there anyway. He was out four horses, worth all told about four hundred dollars, so he could afford to take a chance, he thought as he passed through the Cumberland Gap and on down the Wilderness Road.

Roger's farm, just over the Tennessee line in the Chickasaw Nation, was two days' ride south of Nashville, and the few travelers who made the trip on horseback through Indian and outlaw country, found the farm a convenient overnight stop, so he had heard much about Hughes'.

Some thought the groggery, a few miles out of Knoxville on the Holston River, served its purpose, for if a man had blacks or horses stolen, he might, by throwing out a hint of a reward in Hughes' place, stop them from going east into Virginia or North Carolina.

There were others who hinted that Hughes maintained the place for exactly that purpose, and John Swaney the mailman said it was no place to risk your money at cards.

But Adams kept on. The old bay stud was hardriding but a steady jogger, and he figured to make Knoxville sometime the next day, not allowing for outlaws. Anyway, the stations were close along there, and he didn't look for much trouble.

Trouble never had worried him much anyway. A man who had come West in 1783, practically in the footsteps of Dan'l Boone, and had taken up tomahawk rights along the Trace, never borrowed trouble. Sometimes it caused delay, but a man out there in the almighty wilderness had more time than anything else.

He rode into Knoxville on a Sunday, and it was, if anything, worse than the tales told about it—certainly different from fifteen years before. Some houses were log, some lumber, set anywhere without regard to being square with the world. The streets were fetlock-deep in mud, and even though it was Sunday the grog shops were wide open, with a hell of a lot more singing coming from them than out of the churches—if there was a church.

Men were jostling and swearing. Women yelled from doorways. Half-naked black kids played banjoes while the crowds whooped and danced around them. There were leather-shirted frontiersmen, hard-eyed gamblers, blanketed Indians.

Roger Adams observed all this and quietly rode the stud down the middle of the street, his long rifle across his saddle, his skinning knife at his hip, and his tomahawk slapping at his side.

A fat man stumbled backward out of an open door and sat down in the mud with a splat. A woman looked out and called him names worthy of a flatboatman; the fat man, drunk and slipping back into the mud when he tried to get up, answered back with a mighty string of oaths that very nearly coagulated the atmosphere. Inside, somebody was sawing on a fiddle, and men and women were dancing.

Roger Adams had no feeling about the rightness or wrongness of it. He noted that Knoxville appeared to be all its reputation had proclaimed it, and turned the stud to pick its way around the fat man. Farther on he hailed a staggering group of three men, "Which way is Hughes' Groggery?"

One glared owlishly at him. "Turn right at John Miller's butcher shop and follow the trail to the Holston River. When they hold a bloody knife at your throat, that'll be Hughes', no mistake."

Roger Adams approached Hughes' place without any particular feeling. It was no concern of his how many outlaws headquartered there, so he could get a bee on his horses before they got out of reach. A man couldn't go traipsing all over the East.

Three horses were tied to the hitch rail in front of Hughes' place, and Adams gave them a sweeping look before he dismounted. They were Kentucky horses, probably bred from blood stock, better than the one he rode. He got down, wrapped the reins around the rail, balanced the long rifle in his left hand, and stepped for the door of the groggery, his moccasins squishing out the mud from under his feet.

He was a tall man. Some would have called him thin, but he had wide shoulders, and years on the frontier had put the toughness and suppleness of a young oak tree into his body. He walked easily and confidently, but it was a mark of his forest training that the fringes of his wraparound buckskin shirt, though a full six inches long, hardly lifted at his step, and consequently made no sound.

He heard voices and pushed open the door. Three men were seated at a puncheon table playing cards. All, like Adams, wore coonskin caps with the snouts above their foreheads and the tails down their backs. Adams glanced at them and then at the heavy-bodied man who stood by the table, one foot up on a section of log that served as a stool. This latter was a big man, with brown hair, long uncombed and as long uncut, until it hung down inside his collar like a beaver plew. This man turned to look at him, and Roger stopped, shocked. His first impulse was to leave, but the man stared at him, and he knew he had to go on with it.

"Lookin' for vittles?" asked the man.

"Is this Hughes' place?"

"I'm Hughes."

He was Hughes! His name was some different from 1783. Adams looked around the room, trying to gather his wits. The man had some bolts of cloth, axes and saws, and a counter with hoecakes piled high.

"Four shillings, sixpence for a meal with toddy," said Hughes.

Adams hesitated. The man didn't seem to recognize him. "How much for spirits?" he asked finally.

"Four shillings a bottle."

Adams dropped the butt of his rifle on the rough wood floor. "How much water in it?" he asked.

"It'll sink tallow," Hughes answered.

Adams nodded. Hughes lumbered across the floor to a wicketed corner. He went behind the wicket and passed out a bottle with one hand while he took the money with the other. He examined the milled Spanish peso. "Ye didn't come from the East, with this kind of money."

"I've got land down on the Trace."

Hughes, his head forward, scanned him from under heavy eyebrows. "Ye'll need a place to sleep then?"

Adams hesitated.

"Ye can sleep in the loft for a shilling. Hay and oats for your horse, another shilling."

"All right. Let me have a bottle of beer too."

Hughes pulled the cork. Adams was dry, and drank half the bottle at the first pull. "Make this slop yourself?" he asked.

Hughes' eyebrows flickered up. "Best beer in Tennessee," he said. "Imported from Baltimore."

Adams' legs were wide apart, one elbow high and resting on the muzzle of his rifle. "Down the Trace," he said, "we wouldn't give that to the niggers."

He saw the man's shoulders hunch up, and a glint came in his eyes, but Adams waited.

"Lookin' fer trouble?" asked Hughes.

Adams was temporarily amused, for he wondered what Hughes would do if he said yes. But he didn't say it, for any man who had lived on the frontier long enough to be known on the Trace had something in him besides turnip greens—and Adams was looking for trouble only as it was connected with his search. "I'm lookin' for horses," he, said. "One saddle, three work. The saddle is a chestnut, good blood. The work animals are two duns and a roan with a blaze. Seen anything like that around here?"

Hughes' eyebrows lifted. "Horses come and go. Any brands?"

"RA connected on left hip—except the chestnut. He came up from Spanish country and had the Tres Cruces."

"Might pass the word around. Any reward?"

Adams took a deep breath. Reward money was against his principles, but he knew the value of horses in western Tennessee. "Five dollars apiece—twenty-five for the four of them."

"Not in no North Carolina paper, I hope."

"No paper," said Adams.

He watched Hughes eye him with new interest—as he had expected. But the talk took a sudden turn.

Hughes leaned over. "Ain't I seen you somewhere?"

Adams hesitated for just a moment, but he knew it was too long. Hughes' gray-blue eyes were boring into him. Adams looked back. The lids drooped a little over his own eyes, and he said levelly, "If you did—"

Hughes was frowning. "A long time ago, maybe." He reached for a bottle of beer, so occupied by his thoughts that he moved like an automaton. "Back before the war. Something to do with the British." He turned around. You'd of been younger then—sixteen, seventeen."

Adams drank the beer. "You want to look for my horses," he said, "or my ancestors?"

Hughes' shoulders hunched. Adams didn't move. It was 1798, and two hundred thousand men had poured across the mountains into Kentucky and Tennessee. A good many had reasons for leaving the East, and a man didn't inquire too much too fast.

Hughes said, "All right. Take your horse around back and I'll feed him."

Adams walked out. He turned at the door. The three men at the card table were watching him, and Hughes, still behind the bar, was studying. Well, he'd figure it out all right, Adams thought as he closed the door, but it wouldn't make so much difference here. It would make a difference along the Trace, but not up here. Still, he hoped it wouldn't get around until he'd found his horses.

There was no mistaking Hughes. Adams would never forget that night the man had appeared out of the swamp to report to Dan Morgan and had come face to face with him. Hughes had recognized him then, right enough, and Adams had barely gotten away with his skin.

So thinking, Adams unwrapped the reins. The stud backed away from the rail, and Adams got into the saddle. Two men were galloping down from Knoxville. They pulled up in front of Hughes' place, jumped off, and tied their horses. Both were big men. One was over six feet, the other shorter; both heavy-bodied, with surly faces. The big one had black, curly hair that came low over his eyes. The smaller one looked the same except he was red-headed. Taken all the way around, they were a fine-looking pair of outlaws, Adams figured, and pondered something else as he kicked the stud around the corner of Hughes' big cabin: in a country where a coonskin cap was the badge of a white man, these two were bareheaded. And still something else: the buckskin hunting shirt of the smaller man was torn under the left breast as if by a knife blade, and the edges of the leather were black, as if with blood.

He turned the stud into the stable and walked back to the front of the place to look over the newcomers' horses. He hadn't seen the animals before, but he had seen one of the saddle blankets. He had bought it from a Choctaw Indian about three months before, and it had been on the chestnut when that horse had been taken. He recognized the blanket by its odd design, and, as he did, hardness flashed through him and he took a step toward the door. But then he checked himself. These men might have bought it from somebody else. If they had, they would know where the horses were, and for twenty-five dollars they would help him find them. He slowed down as he approached the door.

Hughes was talking intently to the two men, and as Adams entered, the shorter man turned and stared him full in the face, as if to burn his features in his brain.

Adams closed the door quietly behind him. He still carried the rifle balanced in his left hand. He stared back at the the shorter man and then walked over to watch the card game. One of the men who they called Johnson was drunk; he was winning and was stuffing money into the wallet formed by his wraparound shirt. Adams looked up quickly and saw the two men watching him, and he didn't like the slow, deadly gleam in their eyes.

He had gotten himself into a thieves' nest, no doubt, but it was getting on toward dark and he would have to stick it out. He was glad of one thing: he hadn't brought his son Jeff with him. Jeff liked these wild ways too much. He would have liked it here.

The two surly-faced men had some beer and left.

Johnson looked up at Adams. "Know them?"

Adams shook his head.

"Them are the Harpes—Big Harpe and Little Harpe—Micajah and Wiley."

"Who are the Harpes?" Adams asked pleasantly.

Johnson hiccuped. "Farmers, some say, over on Beaver Creek. But what kind of farmers have three wives for two men?"

Hughes had gone back into his wicket cage.

"It could be a handy arrangement, I suppose," said Adams.

"A man's wives are his own business," one of the other men said.

"This here's a God-fearin' country, ain't it, Metcalf?" Johnson demanded.

"There's some," the third man said, "who don't think so."

Adams was where he could watch the wicket cage without turning his head, and he saw that Hughes was staring at Johnson.

But Johnson was set to argue. "There ain't enough wimmen to go around anyway—and what kind of heathens is it that keep an extra wife to use when they want her?"

"You better not talk so loud," said Metcalf. "Them Harpes are bad Injuns."

Hughes came heavily across the floor with a big candlestick which he set in the center of the table. "They're bad and that's right," he said. "They just escaped from Edward Tiel's posse."

"What was Tiel after them for?" asked Adams.

Metcalf said shortly, "Horse stealin'."

Johnson got up. "I been here long enough. I got all your money," he said. "I'm goin'."

Nobody tried to stop him. He took a rifle from the corner and went out. Adams heard him swearing at his horse as he had trouble getting into the saddle.

Adams looked at Hughes. "Want a game?" he asked.

Hughes glanced at him, and Adams knew from the brevity of it that Hughes had placed him, and he thought Hughes had told Little Harpe about him. But those things could wait. There was a night to pass in this place, and Adams proposed to pass it safely. He chose a bench where he could have his back to the wall while Hughes lumbered back to the wicket cage for money.

The two Metcalfs glanced at each other and got up. Without a word they went outside.

Hughes came back with a small bag of coins. Adams nodded at the door. "Couple of highwaymen?" he asked.

Hughes untied the rawhide whang around the neck of the sack. "My wife's brothers." He spread out the coins. "Don't ye like their looks?"

"It looks to me like they went out to wait for me," Adams said, bringing a bag of coins out of the wallet formed by his lapped-over buckskin shirt. "They may have a long wait."

In fact, he felt sure of it, for he had no intention of going outside until it was light again. The two Harpes were out there somewhere, and he had no doubt either one of them would slit a man's throat for his boots. Johnson had pulled out too; he looked harmless enough, but it was nothing to risk a man's neck on. And now the two Metcalfs had scattered. Quite a crowd there in the dark, Adams thought—and this Hughes was no man to trust if you valued your hair. But Hughes was in front of him, and Adams intended to see that he stayed there all night.

"I'll split a bottle of Monongahela with you," said Adams.

Hughes looked up. Then he arose from a-straddle a log-section stool and went to the wicketed corner. He came back and slammed a heavy bottle down in the center of the table next to the candle.

Adams picked some coins out of his buckskin bag and tossed them over.

Hughes picked up the greasy deck of cards the three men had left. "What'll you play—faro?"

"Not by a damn' sight. I'll play twenty-one—and a two-card twenty-one takes the deal."

Hughes glowered at him for a moment, then began to shuffle. "Make your bet."

Adams slid out a big Spanish peso. Hughes slapped the deck on the table. Adams cut. Hughes picked them up, and Adams said, "Burn one."

Hughes said, "Ye play cards like a damned Tory."

Adams watched him pick them up. He didn't bite at the probing insult. "I've played cards before," he said quietly. "Deal from the top."

Hughes scowled at him over the candle. He dealt two cards apiece.

"I'll stand," Adams said.

Hughes turned up his own cards, a queen and a six. He drew a third—a seven, and groaned: "What have you got?" he asked as he slapped down a peso.

"Does it make any difference?" asked Adams. "You bursted." As a matter of fact, he had stood on a pair of fours, and he didn't want Hughes to know it.

Hughes dealt again. . . . By midnight the deal had changed hands a dozen times, and Adams was eighty dollars ahead.

"Ye are a damned shark," Hughes complained.

Adams didn't answer. He was dealing again. Presently the two Metcalfs came in and went through a door in the back. Adams watched them without moving his head. "They aren't very patient, are they?"

Hughes reared back. "Are you trying to start trouble?" he demanded.

Hughes was in ill humor from his losses. He had tried to change the game, but Adams had stuck to the one game that gave him an even break. Now he watched Hughes start the deal, and said, "If I start it, I will expect to finish it."

Hughes looked uncertain. Adams put both hands in sight on the edge of the table. Hughes burned a card and began to deal. . . .

By four o'clock in the morning they were on their second quart of rye, and Adams held I.O.U's for nearly two hundred dollars. Hughes wanted to quit.

"Cash my notes," said Adams, "and I'll quit."

Hughes took a deep breath. "I haven't got that much money except for banknotes, which you won't accept."

"We like hard money, down on the Trace. Are you standing?"

By daylight Hughes owed him over four hundred dollars. Adams finished the last of the rye and said, "If anybody's waiting out there for me now, I can see them." He drew back from the table. "Cash me in."

"I haven't got that much money," said Hughes.

"What are you playing for, if you can't pay?"

"I—well—"

"You don't figure on losing. Is that it?"

"That ain't what I said."

Adams got up. "It's what I said." He put his fingers around his rifle barrel. "I'm going into Knoxville," he said. "I'll be back by midmorning and I want my money."

Hughes whined. "You'd take a man's bread out of his mouth."

Adams answered, still without apparent emotion, "It's your house and your cards—and you're a professional gambler. I want my winnings—as you would have wanted yours."

"I don't know where to raise that much money."

"See the Metcalfs. See the Harpes; they look like they could raise money in a hurry. Or see Johnson. He had a fistful when he left." Adams thrust the now heavy bag into his shirt, hefted his rifle with his left hand, and went out. He went around to the back and found the stud. He threw on the saddle and tightened the girth. He rode back over the trail to Knoxville.

It was a dead town that morning. Not even smoke showed from a chimney, though the morning was crisp, and he reckoned everybody had stayed up all night like himself. He turned the stud toward a livery stable. He got off at the wide gate that was fastened with a piece of rawhide and a stick. The animals inside were grinding corn with their molars, and swishing their tails against the flies. The place stank with droppings.

Adams tied the reins to the gate and hammered on a side door with the butt of his skinning knife. A grizzly-bearded man finally opened the door, grumbling.

"I want to hire a team and wagon and a man to help," Adams said pleasantly.

"You ain't goin' over the Wilderness Road. It ain't wide enough for a wagon."

"No, I'm going to Hughes' Groggery. I'll be back by noontime."

"All right, all right." The older man shook his head and looked down at his bare feet. "Reckon I better git some shoe-packs on."

"You better," said Adams.

"Git back there, Jennie." The liveryman took a half-hearted swipe at a stringy-haired girl of ten, who, clad in a buckskin wamus, ducked easily. "Go git Jonathan up. I got a job of work for him."

The girl hid behind her father, and only her bright black eyes were distinguishable. "Who's that, Pa?"

"I never ast his name. Now git movin'."

Jonathan was a big, slow-moving boy who had gone mostly to bcef. Adams left the stud tied to the gate, while he got the reins of the team and drove the wagon out of the stable. He pulled up half an hour later in front of the groggery. He slip-knotted the reins around the foot-iron. "Wait here," he told Jonathan. He went inside and hammered on the table with his knife.

Hughes appeared in the rear door in his hunting shirt, his thick black hair rumpled. "What's up, this hour of the morning?"

"I came for my four hundred dollars," Adams said.

Hughes frowned. Finally he said, "It ain't mid-forenoon yet."

"It's as near to it as your debt is going," said Adams. "What good would another hour do, with you sleeping?"

Hughes yawned. "A man has got to sleep."

"Then you better get back to bed," said Adams, and went to the door. "Jonathan, come in here."

Jonathan came in. "Take out those benches and load them in the wagon," Adams said.

Jonathan picked up one under each arm and started out. Hughes came roaring forward. Adams stood in the middle of the room, his legs wide spread, the rifle in his left hand with its butt on the floor, his right hand free.

Hughes stopped. Jonathan came back in. "Take the table," said Adams.

Hate was in Hughes' eyes, but Adams couldn't stop then. He stood his ground. "You better go get your breeches on," he said, "and hunt up some money."

Hughes ground his teeth, and it made a gritting sound, sharp in the morning air. A woman looked through the doorway behind him. There was the heavy thud of the table in the wagon-bed, and Jonathan came back.

"There's an axe outside," Adams said without taking his eyes from Hughes. "Break the wicket loose from the wall."

Hughes, helpless, retreated. Adams laid down his rifle and helped Jonathan pry the wicket loose. He heard a galloping horse, and as they carried the wicket outside he saw Hughes going in the direction of Knoxville.

The safe was too heavy, and they left it, but rolled out two kegs of whisky and six barrels of beer. They were loading the beer on the wagon when Hughes galloped back. His face was purple with rage. "You done tearin' up my place?" he shouted.

Adams surveyed the wagonload. "I figger we got four hundred dollars worth," he said.

Hughes threw a bag of coins at him. "Here's your money. Now see that you get my stuff back where you found it."

There was quite a crowd around them now, but Adams regarded him coolly. "Since I've already got some help, and the wagon has to be taken back empty, I'll have Jonathan take the stuff inside—but you'll have to put it where you want it."

"You put it where you found it."

Adams folded his arms around his rifle. "Got a mighty short memory. Can't rightly say where each piece goes. Maybe you'd best do it yourself if you want to recognize the place."

Hughes got control of himself, and finally he said, "You got your money. Unload my stuff."

"You heard him, Jonathan. Start tossing 'em down."

They set the lumber and the fixtures and the liquor on the ground. Adams went inside. He smiled a little at the bare room. Then he helped Jonathan move everything inside and stack it along the walls.

They were watched now by thirty or forty silent men, some in moccasins, some in boots; some buckskin-shirted, some in homespun gray; some coonskin caps, some in homemade felt hats. Word got around fast at Knoxville. Here and there was a grin, and Adams guessed that more than one man had trouble collecting from Hughes.

"Everything inside now?" Adams asked Jonathan.

Jonathan nodded.

"Then we better take the wagon back before we run up any more time."

"You got your money and you tore up my place!" Hughes shouted. "You'll be sorry!"

Adams said levelly, "You made a mistake telling me that. Come on, Jonathan, let's get this team back to the livery." He looked around him with the hint of a smile in the corners of his mouth. "That's the easiest a team ever earned its oats," he said.

2 He paid the liveryman and Jonathan from the bag Hughes had given him. There was English and Spanish and French money, and Adams doubted he'd get it counted exactly for quite a while. But he hefted the bag, and it felt like four hundred dollars.

"Know where a man could find some stolen horses?" he asked.

The grizzle-headed old liveryman scratched his head. "What kind of horses?"

Adams told him, and the man said, "I ain't seen any horses like them."

"Would you have any idea where to look?"

"I might have ideas—but they might git you and me both in trouble."

"I've been in trouble before," said Adams.

The old man looked up at him. "I don't know," he said, "and I'm not saying—but there's been talk about the Harpes lately."

"Big Harpe and Little Harpe?"

"That's them."

"Where's their place?"

"Eight miles west on Beaver Creek—but I doubt you'll find anybody there."

"Why?"

"The Harpes was caught with stolen horses, but they got away yesterday."

"Are they the two who have three wives?"

The old man nodded slowly. "No decent way to live."

Adams said slowly, "They'll be going back for the women."

The old man shook his head. "I don't know who you be, but the devil himself wouldn't trail the Harpes into their own stompin' grounds. Them two are killers if ever I laid eyes on a killer."

Adams said thoughtfully, "I saw them both last night —and I think you're right. But I want my horses."

"Whyn't you go see Ed Tiel? He got his own horses back. Maybe he saw somethin' of yours."

"Where does he live?"

"Mile out of town."

"The stud is tired," said Adams. "Want to rent me a horse?"

"Got a good saddle mule."

When Adams pulled into Tiel's place the man was patching harness on the sunny side of the shed. Adams climbed the rail fence, and Tiel studied him. "Somethin' on your mind?"

"I live down on the Trace," said Adams. "I lost four horses a couple of weeks back, and I tracked them this far east."

"Good trackin'," said Tiel, punching a hole with an awl.

"They're good horses—and I don't like to lose a good horse."

Tiel twisted two heavy threads and pulled them through a ball of beeswax. "Any law down your way?"

"Some," said Adams.

"Meaning what you carry in your rifle?"

"Yes."

"We organized last night," said Tiel. "Since we've got no sheriff to protect us from men like the Harpes, we'll do the job. We call ourselves the Regulators."

Adams nodded. "That's what we call ourselves down on the Trace."

Tiel poked a new hole. "What kind of horse you missing?"

Adams told him.

"How old was the chestnut?"

"About five," said Adams.

"Branded?"

"RA connected."

Tiel got up. "I've got your chestnut—but I don't know about the others." He walked out into the long grass toward the creek. "That your hoss?"

Adams watched the sleek horse wheel and turn playfully. "It looks like mine. Got a little blood in him, I think."

"What I figgered."

"How much board do I owe you?"

"A night and a day. You're welcome to it. Might be you can do me a turn sometimes."

"I'm obliged," said Adams.

"This halter was on him, but I took it off so he wouldn't step on the rope. Come along and we'll drive him into the shed."

"What do you know about these Harpes?" Adams asked before he started back.

"Not much. They come here a while back with two wimmen." He spat distastefully. "Then Little Harpe married a preacher's daughter—mighty nice little girl. Don't see why she ever went for a man like Harpe. They began to steal hogs—and pretty soon horses. They had your chestnut with them when we captured them, but we couldn't wrangle horses and watch the Harpes too. They got away—and I predict they'll keep going."

"Where will they go, do you think?"

"On west, up the Road, or even over to the Trace."

"What about the horses?"

"Right now I doubt they'd have anything but saddle stuff. I sent a couple of men to their place last night, but the women were gone. They'll probably meet somewhere around the Gap, I'd say."

"Long as I'm going that way—"

"Them Harpes is poison," Tiel warned.

Adams intended to saddle the chestnut when he got back to the livery, but the grizzled old stableman stopped him. "There's a loose roan with collar marks on the Clinch River northeast of town. Got a strange brand, I hear."

Adams squinted at the sun. "I'll ride up tomorrow and have a look."

He stayed that night in Knoxville. Hughes had made some threats against him, but he wasn't worried. The man was well-known, it seemed, and some suggested that maybe he was in with the Harpes. Maybe, even, he was carrying too much guilt of his own from the war. Adams never had known which side Hughes was on; maybe Hughes didn't want it brought up around Knoxville.

Adams rode the chestnut out the next morning. He found the roan and paid the board bill, and rode farther into the Cumberland Mountains to see if he could locate the other two. But he had no luck, and came back to Knoxville a few days later. Tiel met him at the head of a dozen men. "We're looking for a man named Johnson. Hughes said he was in the groggery at the same time you were."

Adams scrutinized the men and saw their tempers were getting short. "Yes, he left shortly after I came in."

"Where were the Harpes then?"

"They left right after Johnson."

"A man'd steal a horse would choke his mother. Anyway, this Little Harpe has a memory like an elephant—and he and Johnson had words in town the other day. Johnson must of known him back in North Carolina. He called him a damned Tory, and Harpe swore and be damned he'd have Johnson's head for it."

"Johnson was showing money that night," Adams recalled.

"Then he never even got to town," said a man behind Tiel. "When Johnson had money he let everybody know it."

"It sounds to me as if he didn't get far away," Adams suggested.

A young boy galloped up on a gray plughorse. "Mr. Tiel! They found Johnson's body!"

"Where at?" demanded Tiel.

"In the Holston River. Somebody dug out his guts and filled him full of rocks, but he came up anyhow."

Adams rode down to the river with them. Tiel's jaw tightened as he looked at the body. "Turtles been eatin' on him," he said. "Anybody look for his money?"

"It wasn't on him," said a man wearing wet boots.

"Them Harpes did it!"

"Let's get the Harpes!"

"String 'em up! There's got to be some law and order in this country."

"We're Regulators, ain't we?"

"The Harpes are gone," the liveryman reminded them. Hughes came walking from the direction of his groggery. He looked a little wild-eyed, Adams thought. Back of him about ten paces were the Metcalfs. Hughes lumbered up and the group of men parted to let him through. He stood there for a moment looking down at the ripped-open body, which looked like the carcass of a deer that had been gutted and washed. Adams looked up and watched Hughes' face. Muscles showed for a moment at the corners of the man's jaws. Then he raised his head. "That's Johnson," he said.

Edward Tiel said harshly, "We know who it is. Who stuck the knife in his back, is what we want to know."

Hughes looked around at the belligerent men. Most

of them had rifles pointing in the general direction of Hughes' feet. Hughes lost a little color. "He was alive when he left my place last night," he said.

"Who else was in there when he left?"

"My brothers-in-law and—the Harpes—Big and Little Harpe. They were both there."

The accusation was plain. But Tiel turned to Adams, who stood back a little with his elbow on the muzzle of his rifle. "You know more about Hughes' Groggery than anybody in Knoxville," Tiel said, and somebody snickered while Hughes reddened but said nothing. "Were you there when Johnson left?"

"I was there," said Adams.

"Who else was in Hughes' place then?"

Adams answered, "The Metcalfs were playing cards with Johnson. The Harpes had just come in for a drink of beer."

Somebody asked, "Did Johnson have any money?"

Adams looked at the questioner. He knew it was a trap. But one of the Metcalfs, now crowding in close on Hughes, spoke up, "He had been winning from us all afternoon—and he wasn't a man to keep his money under cover."

"No reason," the questioner muttered, "why he should be gutted and sunk in the river."

Hughes swallowed. "The Harpes did it. They left right after him."

Both Metcalfs spoke at the same time. "That's right. The Harpes must of done it. They were watching him show his money."

Tiel turned to Adams. "How long did the Metcalfs stay after that?"

Adams looked at Hughes and saw the threat in Hughes' glowering eyes, but Adams looked back at Tiel and said, "Not very long—but long enough for Johnson to get to Knoxville."

Tiel asked, "Anybody see Johnson's horse—a bay, maybe nine hundred pounds, no shoes?"

Nobody answered.

"Then whoever killed Johnson took the horse too."

The liveryman spoke up. "Johnson gener'ly left his hoss at the stable—but it ain't been in since Sunday morning."

The men had now formed a tight group around Hughes and the Metcalfs, while Adams still stood back, watching.

Tiel spoke out loud and clear. "Gents, I figger this is Harpes' work all right, and we'll catch up with 'em sooner or later. But I got a question to ask Hughes here."

There was sudden silence. Only the staccato rattle of a woodpecker in a hard maple across the river sounded for a moment. Then the ring closed a little tighter around Hughes and the Metcalfs.

Adams watched Hughes and knew the man was rightly worried for his life. These were men with short tempers, men to whom killing was not foreign, either way it went. It wouldn't take much to turn them against Hughes, for they didn't like him anyway. And Hughes knew it. He stood in the center of them, his head lowered, dogged, like a bull at bay.

"Ast him the question," said a voice, and there was silence again except for the woodpecker, which must have been after a mighty fat grub from the rate its bill was working.

"We caught the Harpes that morning," said Tiel, "with horses that didn't belong to them. They got away from us and came straight to your place."

Another silence. A short burst from the woodpecker, and a wild turkey thundered up out of the woods and soared across the river to land in the meadow grass.

"I run a tavern," said Hughes. "It's open to them who have the price. I put up my own money and I take my own chances."

"You sold beer to the Harpes right after they escaped from us," said a man.

Hughes tried a sneer, but it was a little feeble, for he was in no position to sneer, Adams figured. "I don't ask every man who comes in if he has just escaped from a posse," Hughes said. "I don't figure it's any of my business."

He wasn't very consistent, Adams noted to himself, for he had been plenty curious about Adams.

The liveryman argued, "I ain't so sure about this here Hughes. His place is knowed as a rowdy place all over eastern Tennessee. Maybe he worked with the Harpes."

Tiel stared at Hughes. "Maybe you and your wife's brothers were in cahoots on the whole deal." His eyes narrowed. "You lost plenty of money to Adams that night. Wouldn't you of been interested in the money Johnson had?"

"I never robbed nobody," Hughes said doggedly.

"I've heard different ideas on that," said the liveryman.

Hughes was a man at bay. He might have been dangerous, but he wasn't armed, and everybody else was.

"Let's string 'em all up!" said an excited man.

"Nope!" said Tiel. "No mobs. We'll take 'em in to Knoxville and give 'em a trial."

Hughes was pale. "What kind of trial will that be?"

"As fair as you gave Johnson," Tiel said.

The Metcalfs seemed on the point of running as the eyes of the crowd turned toward them, but they thought better of it when they heard some triggers cocked.

When they were on the road to Knoxville, Tiel dropped back to talk to Adams. "We'll need your testimony."

"When is the trial?"

"Tomorrow morning."

"I'll stay over. No hurry."

"D'you think he had a hand in it?"

"I don't know. Hard to tell, with so much robbery and killing and organized bands."

"I never got the feeling the Harpes were much on organization," said Tiel. "I figure they robbed and stole because it was easier than doing their own work."

"There are men," Adams observed, "who kill the

36

same way—because it's easier than leaving a man alive to try to get even."

"Since the war was over," Tiel said, "every man who had any trouble in the East has come to Kentucky and Tennessee. And there was plenty of 'em, what with the bad feeling and names called—Tories and rebels— spies and deserters, man against wife sometimes."

Adams glanced up. Was Tiel looking sharply at him? He didn't know, and he tried to give no indication. "Those who were well set had no reason for coming West," he agreed.

Tiel went forward. "You," he picked out two husky-looking, fierce-eyed frontiersmen, "keep guard over these gents tonight."

A hawk-nosed man asked in a nasal voice, "Where you goin' to keep 'em? We ain't got no jail."

"Tie 'em all together with some hame straps," the liveryman suggested, "and put 'em in the feed room at the stable."

"Good idee," said the hawk-nosed man. "You got some good strong rafters to hang 'em from, too."

The two guards snickered. Tiel held up his arms. "Now, gent's don't do anything that ain't legal."

"These fellers never give Johnson a chance," said one.

"We don't know that," Tiel pointed out. "That's why we're going to have a trial."

There was muttering, and Adams was glad he was not in the shoes of the three accused men.

3 AS IT TURNED OUT, the tempers had cooled off some by the next morning. A fat justice of the peace acted as judge, and the three men, accused of conspiracy to murder Johnson, were represented by counsel. Adams was the chief witness against them, and he watched Hughes' malignant eyes as he testified, well aware that he could offer no real evidence against any of them.

The liveryman, Seth Jones, testified that Hughes' Groggery had an evil reputation, but most of them knew you couldn't hang a man even in Knoxville for no more than that.

The verdict was for acquittal, and the three prisoners were released. They made their way, white-faced, through a double lane of hard-eyed men, and they were careful not to move fast and not to answer any of the taunts uttered against them. They walked back down the road, now dry and hard and badly rutted from wagon wheels and horses' hooves.

But anger smoldered in the eyes of the men who watched them. "Remember," Ed Tiel said, "they had a trial. It's like the jury said, there's no real evidence to connect them with Johnson. The only thing we got against them is that the Harpes hung around there."

There was a moment of quiet as the men watched their backs. Then Seth Jones spoke up suddenly, "All right, they ain't guilty of murder—but what about runnin' with the Harpes? That's common knowledge, ain't it?"

The three men kept going steadily. Adams thought perhaps Hughes' big shoulders hunched in a little, but he wasn't sure.

"I reckon it is," said Tiel, "but you can't do anything to them for that."

"Can't we, though?" Seth demanded fiercely.

"They've been acquitted," Tiel pointed out.

"Acquitted before the law," Seth admitted. "But what about the bar of public opinion?"

"The bar of public opinion has no power of capital punishment."

"Ain't it, though!" Seth turned to the men. "How many were at Valley Forge with President Washin'ton?"

Two hands went up.

"How many were at Cowpens against Tarleton?"

Three hands went up, and Adams drew a deep breath.

"And you, Sam Hornaby"—Seth was standing on his tiptoes to point over the heads of the men —"you was with me when that dirty skunk Cornwallis surrendered at Yorktown. That makes eight of us. I claim that's a workin' majority."

Sam Hornaby shifted his rifle. "We didn't have to have a court trial to find a man guilty of consortin' with the enemy."

"That was war," said Tiel.

Seth put his face in Tiel's face. "Sure *this* is war. It's war against the wilderness, against the Indians, against the outlaws. It's war against every man that lives like a stinkin' vulture off o' other men's toil."

Tiel tried to hold them back. "These men have been acquitted."

"There's no organized law here, and that you know as well as I do! There's only law when we make law."

"That's my vote," growled Sam Hornaby. "When polecats like these here get away, we've got no law whatsoever."

Tiel stood apart from them and raised his rifle at Seth. "I'll shoot your eyes out," he said, "if you make a move. We're tryin' to establish law, and we have got to respect the court's decisions."

"Drop that rifle, Ed," said three voices at once. All of them were behind Tiel. He hesitated. "You're a dead man if you touch that trigger," one of them said.

Tiel took a deep breath. His rifle lowered slowly. "I still protest. You tried these men and they were acquitted. You have no right to touch them."

"We can run 'em out of the country. Boys! Git some ropes. Maybe Hughes is innocent, but his place is guilty. Git some ropes and we'll tear it down!"

The three men heard the crowd break into a run after them. Hughes turned like a bear at bay before an angry pack. The two Metcalfs didn't even look. One ran to the right, one to the left, and they disappeared in the brush. The Regulators separated and passed Hughes on both sides. A man on a horse threw a rope over the chimney of Hughes' place and put his horse at a gallop. The chimney crashed in a jumble of dried mud and sticks and rising dust. The Regulators stood for a few seconds, watching the dust mushroom out. Then a woman appeared. She took one look at the Regulators and cursed them. When they moved toward her, she turned and ran, falling almost at once in her long gray homespun dress. The Regulators waited for her to get up. She went screaming around the corner of the tavern. Seth Jones moved in with a rope and hooked it over the ridge pole.

"Give Seth a hand!" ordered Hornaby, and half a dozen men leaned on the rope. The ridge pole began to crack, and dirt showered down.

Hughes' wife came flying around the corner on a bare-backed gray mare. She met Hughes two hundred yards away and read the riot act to him for a quarter of a mile. "You never made an honest living for me! You run with crooks and swindlers and thieves! You—" Her words were lost in a swirl of dust. She was getting out while the getting was good.

Adams, standing at one side, leaning on his rifle, watched Hughes. The big man stood in the middle of the road, helpless, and watched his place come down, log by log, plank by plank, until it was a pile of wood scattered over an acre of ground. Adams felt a little sorry for him, but when he remembered how Hughes had tried to get out of paying his debt, he wasn't sorry at all. And what of a man who kept company with killers and thieves like the Harpes? Adams turned away. Every country to its own law. Where there was no law, sometimes the punishment was severe, sometimes even unjust. But in a new, raw country, the regular law couldn't keep up with outlaws. A few God-fearing men were needed to make their own law. Sometimes it was harsh, but more often it was deserved. Leastwise, it had to be that way. Who could say that Hughes had not helped in the killing of Johnson?

Likewise, nobody could say he had. But Roger Adams knew of a certainty that the man was dishonest. He'd had no intention of paying his gambling debt until Adams had forced the issue. In such circumstances, maybe it was a right smart thing to chase the man on up the road. If he was an honest man, he'd settle somewhere else and prove it. If he was an outlaw at heart, he'd prove that soon enough. Adams nodded to himself. Hughes' loss was not fatal; in this country he could make it back in a hurry—if he wanted to. There were various ways of making it back, and Adams wondered, at that moment, which way Hughes would take.

The groggery was a scattered pile of debris. Some of the men rolled out a keg of whisky and a tin cup, and began to pass it around. Then Hughes made a mistake. He came storming up the road.

"You tore my place down! You run off my wife! What right have you got to drink my whisky?"

Sam Hornaby looked at Hughes through narrowed eyes. "Gents," he said loudly, "we're Regulators, ain't we?"

A chorus of yeses and a couple of Indian yells

answered him. "I say this polecat got off too easy. He ain't whupped yit. He's standin' up on his hind legs actin' like a man. What do you say, gents?"

Seth Jones, with the cup at his lips, stopped to stare. "Then I say let's whup him!"

Hughes saw his mistake. He turned to run, but they swarmed over him.

Seth Hornaby roared, "Roll out a beer barrel!"

Tiel, tight-lipped, came to Adams. "What can we do? They're like madmen!"

Adams answered. "D'you blame them? They know he's guilty of plenty, even though they couldn't pin him down for Johnson's murder. The fool shoulda been grateful for getting away with a whole hide, but you see how it was. He didn't feel chastened. He still wants to fight. I'd say let them take it out of him."

"I reckon there's nothing else to do," Tiel said hopelessly.

Roger Adams said unemotionally, "Unless you want to be laid across that barrel yourself."

Hughes was struggling, but half a dozen men had him, and he should have saved his strength. Sam Hornaby faced him across the beer barrel. "We aim to give every man satisfaction," he said. "We'll whup you till you've had enough."

"You've got no right to whip me!"

"We're takin' that right," Sam Hornaby said softly.

"We'll keep it up till you say we've got the right," Seth Jones declared.

Roger Adams shifted his rifle and frowned. "It may

43

be little bloody," he told Tiel. "That Hughes feller strikes me as a mite stubborn."

"Stubborn as hell," muttered Tiel. "They'll have to cut him to ribbons."

"It's been done before," said Adams. "Tarleton's men—" He didn't finish.

"You was in the war?" asked Tiel.

Adams nodded, but he did not offer more explanation, and Tiel did not ask. He looked away after a moment.

They stripped off Hughes' homespun shirt and his woolen pants. They flung him on his stomach across the barrel. They tied a short rope to his left foot and ran it under the barrel to his right hand, and pulled it tight. They connected his left hand and right foot the same way. Then they stood back from the naked man for a moment. The sun shone down on his white skin. The woodpecker was hammering away again, and the cloud of dust from the demolishment of the groggery began to envelop the group around Hughes.

"Pull him out into the open," said Seth Jones. "I don't want to make a mistake and hit the barrel."

"He's a man anyway," said one.

"Was you curious?" asked Seth.

"It don't hurt to make sure."

"What's the difference?"

"There's a heap—in case you didn't know."

Seth Jones said scornfully, "I had kids before you was born. I can look at that hind end a mile away and tell it ain't no woman."

Sam Hornaby was making knots in a three-quarter-inch rope. "How many'll we give him?" he asked.

"Till he hollers enough!"

Sam looked scornful. "What if he hollers first time?"

"Give him a hundred!"

Sam shook his head. "He won't last a hundred."

"Make it fifty," said Seth Jones. "From then on it's up to him."

"Fifty," said Hornaby, "and the first man who lays on an easy one gets five on his own rump."

Sam straightened up. He was a tall man, and tough like a weathered oak. He stepped back from Hughes and measured his distance, feeling the rope in his hands, the end with three knots as big as a man's fist humping itself on the ground like an inchworm. He threw it over his shoulder, came to his toes, and brought the knotted end down on Hughes' naked back with a thud.

Adams saw a spasm of pain go through Hughes' body. The man looked around wildly for help. His eyes met Adams', but Adams didn't move. Then as Sam Hornaby lifted himself again to his toes, Hughes closed his eyes and tensed himself.

The rope left three smears of blood on the man's back where the hard fibers cut through the skin. Still Hughes made no sound, but this time his eyes didn't open. After the blow he lay limp across the barrel. A shadow moved across the ground, and Adams looked up. A buzzard was circling very high in the light blue sky.

Sam gave him three more. The last time, the knots smacked, and blood flew over Hornaby's clothes. "First time I've seen such red blood since I left my tracks in the snow at Valley Forge," he declared, and handed the rope to Seth Jones.

After half a dozen, Seth turned the rope over to a hawk-nosed Virginian.

"I know how to do this," the Virginian said softly. "Tarleton give me thirty-nine onct."

Hughes started to raise his head to look at Adams, but the rope cut into his back. He tried to say something but the knots cracked across his kidneys.

Hughes screamed at the sixteenth stroke, laid on by a young giant in buckskins. His scream rolled up the meadow along the river, and for a moment the woodpecker stopped hammering. Adams looked up again. There were two vultures in the sky.

Hughes screamed at every stroke after that. At the twenty-eighth his back was a bloody mass of torn flesh. At the thirty-seventh his buttocks were indistinguishable and his thighs were covered with blood. At the forty-fourth he quit screaming and could only gurgle, with more blood than saliva running from his mouth.

"Screamed his throat out," Roger Adams observed.

Tiel shook his head. "It's brutal. Men shouldn't do a thing like this."

Adams pointed a thumb at the grave where they had buried Johnson, less than a hundred yards from where he had been found. "Who d'you reckon did that?"

46

Sam Hornaby finished the fifty lashes and tossed the blood-soaked rope aside. Bluebottle flies already were buzzing around the man's bloody back. Adams looked up. There were seven buzzards circling now.

"Untie him," Hornaby said, "and toss him in the creek. That cold water'll bring him to."

He was limp. They threw him in with a mighty splash, and Seth Jones waded in to drag him out so he wouldn't drown. When he came to, choking weakly, they left him with his clothes beside him. Men balanced beer barrels and whisky barrels on their saddles and rode back to town. Hughes didn't even raise his head.

"They took it out of him," Adams said.

Tiel shuddered. "Awful way to treat a man."

Adams said tightly, "Plenty of those men have got scarred backs from that same treatment. Is it so strange that they would want turn about?" He moved to his horse. "You better see that he gets dressed. The buzzards—"

"I'll see," said Tiel.

Roger Adams rode back to Knoxville not exactly easy in his mind. It was true that the man known now as Hughes had always been a man of dubious loyalties. It was true also that he had changed his name and tried to start over, but retribution had caught up with him. He remembered Hughes' wife leaving the groggery. Was it impossible to start over, to make a home where a man's family would have safety? Couldn't a man leave his past and make a fresh, clean start in a new country, or was it destined always to be a dark and bloody ground for those who had come to it from violence?

The liveryman came out of the stable as Adams pulled up. "Just heard there's a couple of duns up the Holston. Feller name of Williams took 'em in. Might be you should go have a look."

"How far is it?"

"Only about a day's ride."

"I've come this far," said Adams, "I may as well finish the job."

The old man came up and put a hand on the saddle-horn. "You talk uncommon good for a man in this country."

Adams eyed him, but kept his face calm. "I was raised well," he said, and added, "I think I'll ride the chestnut up the river."

He was gone three days, but found no trace of the duns. On the fourth morning he rode back to see Edward Tiel. "Has there been any sign of the Harpes' coming back?"

"Not a bit," said Tiel. "I rode by their place once, and Seth Jones was out there, but the cabin is deserted. The women picked up and left."

"Was there horse sign?"

"Plenty. The horse pen had been well-used, and horses had been tied out in the woods. More horses than the Harpes ever owned."

"Still, it doesn't sound as if my workhorses were among them, for the women wouldn't be driving horses if they were trying to escape."

"Way it looks to me," said Tiel. "I'm afraid your duns are gone unless you're lucky."

Adams swung into the saddle. "Two out of four is a good return."

"I hear you won four hundred dollars from Hughes."

"Winning was easier than collecting."

"Stay and have dinner," Tiel suggested. "We killed a hog two days ago. Been hanging up long enough to get frostbitten."

Adams looked at the sun to conceal his awareness of that incessant curiosity about a man's past. If he stayed there'd be questions, either direct or implied. "Sorry," he said. "I've got to get ready to take out for home. I figure on leaving in the morning."

"Anything I can do," said Tiel, "let me know."

"I will." He rode out of the farmyard. Tiel had a right nice little place, with half a dozen small children running around in ankle-length wamuses. He wouldn't mind getting better acquainted with Tiel if the man could keep a checkrein on his curiosity. But that never happened. Sooner or later somebody wanted to know what you had done in the war.

He sat in a monte game that afternoon. He won and lost, and at midnight he was ahead a bottle of whisky and behind about eighteen dollars. He went back to the livery and rolled up in his blankets in the loft. The hay made a softer and better-smelling bed than any he had seen in Knoxville, and he was sound asleep in no time.

He left early the next morning, riding the chestnut, leading the stud and the roan. The road from

49

Knoxville wound up into the mountains toward the Gap. He went through the Gap and down toward Barboursville. Far ahead of him he saw a man in a large greatcoat walking slowly.

The man didn't turn. Adams pulled up alongside. The man turned, and Adams' eyes narrowed as he looked at Hughes.

The man stared at him and at the horses. "I need a ride," he said.

Adams did not answer immediately.

Hughes said, "You've got an extra horse. I'll ride the stud."

"Where are you going?"

"To Nashville—and if you don't let me use your horse, I'll tell everything I know about you."

"Tell and be damned," Adams said quietly.

"You're bluffin'," said Hughes. "Do you want to face men like Sam Hornaby and have him know you were with Tarleton?"

"I deserted Tarleton and joined Morgan."

"A dirty British spy," said Hughes. "You deserted Morgan a week later."

"I left because you would have accused me of being a spy. There was nothing else I could do."

"Your name was Ashby, back in England. Your old man has an estate as big as Jefferson County. Is it reasonable ye'd give that up?"

"It might not seem so to you. It might to me."

"Will any man in the West believe a wealthy Tory would give up his inheritance?" Hughes insisted.

50

Adams drew a deep breath. "I'm inclined to give you a lift out of common humanity," he said, "but I don't like to be threatened."

"I don't make threats I can't back up," said Hughes, and Adams knew now he wasn't bluffing. "I've told Little Harpe all about you. If anything happens to me, he'll spread the word down on the Trace, where you live. How long do ye think your neighbors will drink out of the same horn with ye then?"

Adams felt a sudden sinking. This was the thing he had most dreaded for fifteen years: that his true past would become known, that he had been a member of Tarleton's infamous dragoons. It wouldn't help to say that he had been in the unit only a few months; that he had deserted when he saw what Tarleton was like. There were in Kentucky and Tennessee men with backs like Hughes', men whose wives and daughters had been outraged in Tarleton's camps. These men would find it easy to remember and quick to avenge.

Adams' skinning knife was in his right hand. He tried the keen blade with his left thumb, while Hughes watched, his shoulders suddenly hunched again. Adams felt a deep scorn for him.

"Get on the stud," he said harshly, "before I cut your throat."

4 THEY RODE INTO STANFORD the next day, and stopped at a tavern for food. The tavernkeeper was a man with gray muttonchop whiskers. "Have you heard the news, gents?" he asked.

"What news?" asked Adams, throwing out a coin.

"Best news Kentucky has had yet. The Harpes have been captured."

Adams moved his eyes to look at Hughes. "What did they do?"

"They killed a young fellow from Virginia named Langford. Dirty shame too. Langford had bought breakfast for all of them—two men and three wives. He took pity on them and that's how they paid him back. Some fellers driving cattle found him. The cattle smelled the body. Now they've got the whole bunch— and there's some say the Harpes have killed others. Spirits you'll have?"

Adams nodded. Hughes hardly moved. They had their drink, and Hughes paid for his own.

"You aren't broke," said Adams.

"I owned the land, and I had some money in the safe. I would of been all right," Hughes said with unexpected bitterness, "if you hadn't of turned the town against me that way."

"You'd have been all right," Adams, "if you had paid your just debt. What did you expect me to do—

leave Knoxville with you owing me? You wouldn't have let me go if I had owed you."

Hughes scowled.

Adams said over his second glass of rye, "You would have been all right if you hadn't kept the company you did."

"You forgot what I told you," Hughes muttered.

"Maybe it's a thing to be forgotten." But he was bluffing again; it was a thing you couldn't altogether leave behind. "Do you feel like offering help to the Harpes now?"

Hughes glowered. Their food came—fried mush and ham and a mug of coffee. Adams watched Hughes as he ate. Would it be safer to kill the man when he got a chance? Hughes said he had told Little Harpe about Adams' service with Tarleton—but what if Hughes turned up missing farther down on the Trace, in another legal district? Well, it could be done—but wasn't that the way of outlaws, to take the law into their own hands? This was a country where sometimes honest men *had* to take the law into their hands, because the outlaws moved too fast for legal proceedings—but that was for the public benefit. This would be for his personal benefit—and there was a difference.

He thought about it quietly while they ate, and he wondered how it would be to travel with Hughes for a week. He wondered what he would do if Hughes insisted on going with him down on the Trace. It was hard to know. When he faced the situation, he would doubtless solve it. That was about all he could know now.

They slept together in the loft of a farmer's cabin that night. Adams did not know whether Hughes had a knife, but presently the big man, lying on his stomach, for his back must still have been raw, began to snore. It was the middle of December, and Adams pulled a buffalo robe over him as the blaze in the fireplace below died down. He went to sleep rather quickly, and it seemed only a moment later that he was awake. He opened his eyes but did not move. All was quiet down below. The farmer and his wife and three children were sound asleep. The fire was dead. Moonlight came through the greased deerskin that served as a window, and illuminated the room with a ghostly glow that showed mostly shadows and darker shadows.

It was pitch dark in the loft. His senses came alert. He lay there a moment more, but felt no motion in the cabin. An owl hooted outside; a wolf howled somewhere off in the canebrake. It was cold. Adams decided that he had awakened because of it, and was just about to pull the buffalo robe around his shoulders when he froze in the thought of it. Hughes, at his side, was turning over slowly, stealthily.

Adams waited. He began to breathe a little deeper, and at the same time, when Hughes moved again, his own hand went to the handle of his knife.

He thought about it for a moment. He didn't want to be brought into the open, which was bound to happen if they got into a fight that would wake up the farmer. Nor did he want a butcher knife in his back.

The next time Hughes began his slow partial turn, Adams pressed the point of his own knife in Hughes' direction until it hit something and stopped. He whispered, "Drop that knife, Hughes, or I'll slit you open."

The man seemed to stiffen for a moment. Then there was a dull thud as a knife fell on the buffalo robe. Adams took a deep breath. He had awakened just in time. The man had raised his arm for the kill. . . .

They had dodgers, bacon and coffee the next morning, and the farmer's wife asked them brightly, "Did you sleep good last night?"

Hughes grunted. Adams, with the extra knife now hidden under his belt, said, "Yes, ma'am, very well."

"Your eyes look a little red," she said. "Maybe it's the water."

"Or the wind. The wind was bad yesterday," said Adams. He had not slept after he had taken the knife away from Hughes, for he knew the man might have had another one. And still might.

"More coffee?" she asked. "We just got some yesterday from the Falls at Louisville."

"No, thanks," said Adams. She was a plain little woman, and likely didn't have much company, and she was anxious to please, but Adams knew how precious coffee was. One cup a week was all most families ever had. He paid her and took his rifle. He would have liked to buy a bottle of rye or a pint of peach brandy,

55

but he didn't dare; a man had absolutely to play the pauper anywhere in the West. The least sign of more money than he had to have might bring him a killing.

Then he remembered the money he had in his shirt—nearly seven hundred dollars all told that Hughes knew about. Hughes, he had no doubt, would kill him for that if nothing else. They were working south toward Nashville, and Adams began to plan to get rid of the man. But he needn't have worried, for Hughes took off before they reached Nashville. Adams waited for him after dark that night, but the man didn't come in. Adams went to look for him. He and the tavernkeeper carried pitch pine torches and looked in the barn. The stud and Hughes' roll of clothes was gone.

"It looks like he lit out," the tavernkeeper said.

"That's the way it looks." Adams stuck the pitch pine into the ground to put it out.

"His own hoss, I reckon."

Adams nodded. The stud was a hard rider, and he was too old to service young mares, so Adams felt it wasn't too much loss.

The tavernkeeper, still holding his torch high, was moving among the horses. "That stud had the same brand as the roan you led in here."

"They came from the same farm," said Adams.

The tavernkeeper looked at him curiously. "Your business," he said. "The feller looked like an outlaw to me."

"Give him time," said Adams. . . .

Nashville was a neat town, in 1798, with a smart number of cabins built of cedar logs, and most of them had mud or stone chimneys. It was a busy place of buggies and wagons that came down the Ohio from Pittsburgh an flatboats. Adams stopped at the Red Heifer Distillery and bought a demijohn of spirits. He went to William Tadd's store and bought ten yards of red and white calico. At Clark's he inquired about the price of coffee. He stopped at the post office for mail, but there was none—nor had he really expected it. He lit out down the Trace, and by dark he had reached Tom Davis' cabin, he swapped gossip and told about the Harpes.

"There's been a powerful lot of trouble along the Trace lately," said Davis. "D'you reckon them Harpes had something to do with it?"

"Hard to say." Adams filled his cob pipe and lit it with a coal held between two twigs. Then he looked up at Davis. "Short on tobacco?"

"I'm chewin'," Davis said.

"The Harpes are bloody killers, but I don't think they've been down here yet. They've been too busy on the Wilderness Road. Good place for 'em down here, though."

"Swaney said they were suspected of other murders."

Adams yawned. "That mail carrier knows everything that goes on—but he may be right." He sat for a while, smoking out his pipe, while Davis chewed and spat into the fire. Mrs. Davis grated corn, and the four children ate raw turnips that had been brought out of the root cellar. Finally Adams knocked out his pipe and went to the ladder.

"There's an extry bearskin in the corner," said Davis. "You may need somethin'. It's gettin' on to Christmas, and tonight's a cold one."

Mrs. Davis looked up. She was angular-faced and her skin was weathered. She set the grater on the puncheon table and straightened her shoulders under the rough gray wool dress. "Man died up there a week ago. Never knew his name or nothin'."

Adams went on up. The heavy wooden bowl was still in Mrs. Davis' lap, and presently he heard her grating corn again.

The next day at noon he crossed the Duck River, the boundary line between Tennessee and the Chickasaw Nation. He turned off of the Trace toward evening, hobbled the horses so they could feed in the canebrake, cached his money high in the bare branches of a persimmon tree, and went back a quarter of a mile from the Trace to a leanto he had used before.

In the morning he shook his gold down out of the tree and went after the horses. The chestnut had wandered off about three miles, and since the roan was not saddle-broke he had to walk, so it was late when he got back on the trail. He ate some jerked beef he had bought at Nashville and some journey cake Mrs. Davis had given him, but he kept the horses moving.

He reached the Tennessee River in midafternoon, and James Colbert, the Chickasaw chief, brought the ferry over for him. They gave him a supper of deer loin, potatoes, and coffee made of roasted acorns, and that night he slept in a big cabin with thirty Indians.

In the morning he was covered with lice. He caught up his horses, thanked the chief, and rode off. At the first creek he came to he took off his clothes, whipped them out thoroughly, and went into the cold water and scrubbed himself with sand. His teeth were chattering before he got through, but he was free of vermin—and it was hard enough to keep the children free of animals without his bringing them.

By noon he reached an oak tree where he found a buffalo horn and blew on it with a sound that would carry through the bottoms for a mile. He rode on, and suddenly the narrow trail, so long hemmed in by forest trees and solid canebrake, widened out. A pack of barking dogs surrounded him, but he rode toward the large cabin. Behind it, in the door of the log kitchen, Marie, their black cook from Santo Domingo, stood in the doorway, eyes wide, white teeth shining, while a brood of black pickaninnies, some of the smaller ones naked, squeezed past her ample skirts to follow the dogs.

The front door of the cabin opened, and Anne stood there barefooted, in a long plain linsey-woolsey dress. He thought, seeing her in the sun, that she was still an uncommonly pretty woman, proud of form and figure, warm and affectionate no matter how hard the day's work. Adams looked over the yard. Three small children with bowl-cropped hair, each dressed in a tow-cloth wamus like an ankle-length nightshirt, and the boy with two slits in his shirt-tail to tell him from the girls, were chasing one another in the maple grove. He heard the ringing of axes, and was relieved that Jeff was at work in the deadening, as he had told them. He never had any doubt about Charles, but Jeff needed watching.

He drew in a deep breath. He had the makings of a good plantation here. A few years to get more land cleared off and get in the first crop of corn so he could put the land to other uses. Some day the government would legalize his title; the Trace would be wide enough for vehicles; outlaws would be cleared out like a nest of cockleburs. There would be a time when there would be a market for their produce and a way to get it to market; the Spanish couldn't close the Mississippi forever. He wondered momentarily how much difference it would make, when they got around to legalizing titles, if they knew he had been a deserter from the British army. Nobody was likely to find out, because nobody but Hughes knew it—Hughes and Little Harpe.

There were only two men, then, who stood between him and this new life—Hughes and Harpe. Could a man live down his old life? Could he escape from a set of circumstances not of his own making but nevertheless dangerous, and start a new life? He thought he could, in this new country—and yet men were moving west every day, and his secret was moving west with them. Hughes, now, was somewhere north of Nashville, if not closer. Would he come south on the Trace?

Roger's teeth parted as he breathed deep of the frosty air. For a moment he felt harried. Then he smelled the hickory smoke under curing hams, yellow soap in a boiling kettle of laundry, and felt reassured. He had come a long way into the wilderness; with his own two hands he had carved out this little plantation, and daily it was growing. He would maintain it against all comers. The neighbors around him had accepted him for what he was, not what he had been; they might be curious but they didn't pry too deeply into a man's past.

He looked again at Anne. She gave a sharp command to the dogs, and they quit barking. He nodded, and rode around the house to the horse pen. He unsaddled the chestnut and put the saddle on the fence; he turned the two horses over to Marie's man, a very black Haitian, who shambled up and said, "Aft'noon, Mr. Adams."

"Any wolves lately, Gene?"

"No, suh. We-all ain't been bothered."

"Put them in the canebrake then."

He untied the package back of the saddle and started for the house.

He noted the big pile of wood alongside the house; Anne had kept the older boys working. He walked inside. The fireplace was opposite the door and would take a log twelve feet long; there was a second door in one end of the cabin through which he could snake a log of that size with a horse or an ox. They were going to build a second cabin for sleeping, but hadn't gotten to it yet. There were several pairs of deer antlers on the walls, and a set of buffalo horns, though there weren't much buffalo down on the Trace any more. There were pegs driven between the logs to hold powder horns, leather coats, saddlebags, and whatever. A big bearskin was on the floor.

On each side of the fireplace was a cupboard to hold their wooden dishes. In one corner of the room was a double-deck bed; the rest slept in the attic. Under the bed was an assortment of gourds for sugar, salt, gunpowder, and coffee. At the side of each cupboard, was a deerskin container hanging on the wall—one holding bear's oil, the other honey, and from the ceiling hung dried apples, pumpkin, beans and gourds filled with nuts.

He hung his bullet pouch on a peg, stood his rifle in a corner. Liz, the oldest girl—she was almost fourteen—was pouring candles, while her mother was cutting fringes on a buckskin shirt that she had made for one of the boys. "Seen Swaney?" Roger asked.

Anne looked up briefly. "Coming up from Natchez, he said there's an outlaw named Mason was chased out of Kentucky, and some people think he's working on the Trace north of Natchez."

Roger laid the package on the table by the candle mold, then went outside, got an axe from the log kitchen, and started for the deadening.

Jeff, who was twelve, was working with a grubbing

hoe, while Charles, who was ten, was using the other axe. The deadening itself was an area of some fifteen acres where all trees less than a foot through had been cut down, while the bigger ones had been girdled and left to die. This piece of ground was four years old, and the upper branches fell readily. Roger surveyed the litter of limbs on the ground and said, "Must have had some wind."

"Had a blow night before last," Jeff said without missing a lick.

They were both good, tall boys with shoulders like his own. When Charles tied in with the axe, he threw a chip as big as a man's hand. Roger picked out an eight-inch limb and went to work. Some good sized stuff had fallen. Well, it needed a lot of wood to keep the cabin warm all winter. He took a cut. This winter, he thought, would be a good time to clear off some more canebrake—cut the cane and grub the roots. There was plenty of time to let it lie for a couple of months; then they'd burn it, and by planting time it would raise the finest corn on the Trace.

They were still swinging their axes when Anne blew the dinner horn. They shouldered their tools and went to the creek to wash. That was one thing Anne had insisted on, and Roger was proud of her, for people on the frontier got pretty careless. It was nothing to see a man eat with dirty hands and then wipe them on his hunting shirt.

Roger sniffed as they came near the cabin. "Smells like a treat for tonight."

"We killed three fat 'possums. They been up on the roof to get frostbit," said Jeff.

They all sat down to the business of eating—for eating was a business in this country. With only a roughhewn wooden table in place of the polished mahogany he had known in England, with wooden plates in place of china, tin cups instead of glass, hunting knives and two-pronged forks with buckhorn handles, and nothing like a tablecloth (for any kind of cloth was hard to come by), a man couldn't be very fussy. He sat down at his place and asked the blessing. Then he looked around. The three little ones, Will, Betty, and Sarah, were in place on one side of the table—the girls like Anne, the boy like him. The two older boys and Liz were on the opposite side; Anne was at the other end. Marie came in with a hollowed-out half-log filled with two baked 'possums and piled high with potatoes.

"We have a new neighbor," said Charles.

"I didn't see any sign," said Roger.

"He's nine miles down the Trace—name of Virgil Coates. Not married, either." He looked slyly at Liz as he said this, and Roger noted with something of a shock that Liz blushed and kept her eyes on her food.

Liz had been a good girl. She was a hard worker like her mother, and caused them no trouble. Nor had she ever indicated any interest in men. That wasn't so astonishing, though, come to think of it. There were no men down here but travelers and outlaws. But now there was a settler, unmarried—and Liz was blushing.

It made Roger feel strangely desirous of protecting Liz, and at the same time strangely helpless. For Liz was growing up; no doubt about that. She was almost as old as her mother had been when Roger married her.

They fell to eating. Presently Will said, "Mr. Swaney told us they have *white* potatoes in Natchez. He said they came on a boat."

Roger hesitated. That meant they were shipping from Ireland, probably. "Don't you like our potatoes?" he asked.

"Sure, I like 'em, but—I like white potatoes too."

Roger smiled, and he realized abruptly that it was the first time he had smiled in two weeks. It was good to be here—temporarily, at least, away from thievery and violence and killing.

Eventually the outlaws, forced farther and farther west, like maybe the Masons right now, would come down the Trace. It was lawless enough already, with so much gold carried back north from New Orleans. That had been going on for fifteen years or more. A farmer shipped a load of corn or furs or whisky down-river to New Orleans on a floatboat; he sold his stuff and came north on the Trace on horseback. A mighty lot of them never reached home; a lot of bodies were never found, for bodies could be buried or cut up or fed to the alligators—and who was there to know, for two years ago there had not even been a mail carrier on the Trace. Now that there was mail, it was to be expected that either the United States or Spain would enforce the law. They were fortunate, Roger thought, for the worst outlaws, like the Harpes, who killed senselessly, were in Kentucky, and with luck they would presently be cleaned out. On the Trace, only travelers with money were in danger.

He picked up his tin cup, and nearly spilled from it, for Anne had filled it with whisky to the brim instead of only half full as usual. He glanced at her. She was looking down at her plate.

5 THE NEXT DAY they started boiling salt. The lick was about three miles back in the forest, in a grove of black willow and swamp oak, and Roger and the two older boys led a team, loaded with tallow and hog blood and what lime was left from the year before, back to the spot before sunup. He put the boys to cutting wood, for wood was the big need. It took seven hundred gallons of water boiled away to make a bushel of salt.

Winter was the time to do it, for there weren't many chores in connection with planting, and besides it was hot work even in the winter. It was hard work, like a lot of other things, but work was work. If a man had a helpful wife and children that minded him, and was able to keep them all fed and warm, what difference did it make what he worked at? Salt shipped in was ten dollars a bushel, which meant he could throw two bushels on a packhorse and take it to Nashville and get a lot of things they needed.

"Where we going to get wood this year?" asked Jeff as they unloaded.

"We better cut into the oaks up the hill there. You can take the roans and use them to drag up a load when you get it cut. Make the pieces about three feet long."

Will spoke up. "Mr. Coates said he'd like to help with the boiling."

Roger hesitated. Coates? Yes, the unmarried man who had moved in nine miles down. Roger looked down at the two boys, and they were both looking at him. He knew they were thinking the same as him: there'd be courtin', with an unmarried man about. But, he sighed, there'd be courtin' anyway, and he might as well get a look at this Coates. If he was a good neighbor his help would be welcome. He looked at the boys without seeing them and said, "You and Betty can go tell him after dinner."

"I know the way by myself," said Will.

"I don't want either one of you to travel the Trace alone. There are too many outlaws in the country."

"You went alone," said Will.

"He's twice as old as you," Charles said scornfully.

"Did you see any outlaws?" asked Will.

Roger said thoughtfully, "I think I slept with one."

"Well," said Jeff, "then he didn't do anything to you." He sounded disappointed, and Roger knew why.

"No—because I had my knife in his stomach first."

"Did you kill him?"

"It wasn't necessary."

"I'd like it better if you killed him."

"You're too bloodthirsty," Anne said severely.

"Get started on the wood," said Roger, and the boys went off.

Roger surveyed the eight large brass kettles they always used. They were set in a row over a narrow ditch that served as a sort of fireplace. You pushed the wood in at one end of the ditch, and the other end served as a flue. He would have to chink up the kettles with clay to keep from losing heat, but that was a small matter. The pits where they got the water were partly filled in, but he dug them out, and was satisfied when they filled promptly with the brackish water. He tasted it and made a face. They'd have no trouble getting salt out of that stuff. He filled the first kettle with a wooden bucket, and the pit filled as fast as he could carry the water. The kettles held twenty-five gallons each, and he had worked up a fair sweat by the time he got them all filled.

By that time the boys were bringing in their first load of wood. When Anne's horn blew for dinner, they had a good stack of oak cordwood and were firing. On the way to the cabin Roger said, "Tell our neighbor we'll start up in the morning—and get back here right away. You know what an almighty lot of wood it takes to make salt."

Anne and Liz, barefooted even in the cold, had been washing clothes, for he had heard their battling boards most of the morning, and now they were hanging out clothes on the brush to dry.

"We'll need half a dozen good gourds to ladle," Roger said to Anne.

She looked at him through half-lowered eyelids, and he knew she was thinking of last night, and he smiled. Anne was a wife. He wondered if Liz would be like her. If she was, this fellow Coates had better be decent to her.

69

"I'm sending the boys to invite our neighbor to help," he said so Liz could hear. He caught his wife's smile, and knew he hadn't been wrong about Liz's blushing.

The next morning Virgil Coates came into the clearing on horseback, almost before the sky lightened over the forest to the east. Enterprising young fellow, anyway, Roger thought to himself as he pulled on his leggings and moccasins. He went outside. The dogs had surrounded the newcomer, who still sat his horse, waiting for an invitation to alight. Good manners, too, Roger thought.

"Morning, stranger. 'Light and come in. There's fried mush and potatoes and some possum left over from last night."

"I had my breakfast," he said, "but I'll sit with you."

Coates walked his horse over to a stump. Roger called off the dogs. "I brought along some tallow," Coates said.

"We can always use it." Roger went outside and made sure the door was closed. "We can work on shares," he said. "I furnish the kettles and five hands, two boys and a girl. I figure about one bushel out of six to you."

Coates got down. He wasn't as tall as Roger, but well set up and handled himself well. About twenty-five years old, Roger judged.

"Sounds fair," Coates said, and tied his horse.

Roger rubbed his horse's neck, noting its looks. It was a good horse, nothing fancy, all-around—plow or saddle. Another point in Coates' favor.

"I hear you're alone," said Roger.

Coates looked up soberly. "Yes, I'm alone."

"Just come West?"

"No, I been West quite a while."

"Red Banks?"

"No. Harrodsburg."

"What kind of business you in up there?"

"Had a little farm."

"You didn't like it up there?"

"I did until lately. The Harpes killed my wife and baby."

Roger stroked the horse's neck. "Sorry. I thought the Harpes were in jail."

"They are—but I don't figure they will be long. Anyway, plenty of things are coming out now that they did before they got Langford."

"They'll surely hang."

"They won't be able to keep them long enough," Coates predicted. "There's no jail in Kentucky that could hold two men like them."

Roger led the way into the house. He had asked a lot of questions, but he had found out what he wanted to know, and Coates hadn't resented it—which was good, for, oddly enough in this country of men with varied pasts, curiosity was ever-present and even annoying, and it spoke well for a man not to resent questions. Roger wished that he himself could answer questions with the steadiness of Coates.

Anne and Liz, barefooted as always, went to the lick and divided up the work.

Roger chose the job of keeping the kettles filled, and

took off his moccasins to work barefooted, for moccasins were a nuisance in wet ground. Liz struck a fire with flint and steel and elected to feed the furnace. Anne would handle the brine, for as the kettle nearest the flue end got low in liquid, water from the one next to it, already well-evaporated, would be ladled into it for crystallization. In this manner the partially evaporated water was passed along from one kettle to another, to reach its final stage usually in the last kettle. Anne was expert on the use of blood and lime and tallow to crystallize the salt and bring it out fine and white.

Coates went off up the hill with the boys, and presently, with axes still ringing, Charles came back with the first load of wood. It was still before sunup.

"Mr. Coates knows which end of the axe is the cutter," said Charles, dragging his load into place.

"Hump!" said Roger, coming up with two more pails of water. A father had nothing to say about his daughter any more—not even when she married.

Then he reminded himself that he was getting his saddle on backwards, for nobody even knew if Virgil Coates was interested in getting married again. Feeling on the frontier was strong against any marriageable person staying single any longer than necessary, for living took more work than one could manage unless he was eccentric or a "long hunter." Life on the frontier was hazardous too, and since neither men nor women could be sure of tomorrow, there was a feeling that a day wasted was a day lost.

When they started back to the house for dinner, Roger saw Coates' eyes briefly on Liz, and knew then that Coates was no long hunter; it was only a question of time—certainly no longer than early spring, for they'd have to have a house-raising before planting time. Once planting started, there wouldn't be any house-raising, except in case of fire.

Roger stayed at the kettles to keep the fire going. He could hear them returning, and he was sitting on the woodpile for a minute, when he saw a black bear shamble across the edge of the lick. Without getting up, he reached silently for his rifle, took aim across the kettles, and put a lead slug just behind the bear's shoulder. It growled a couple of times, then stretched out on its back.

Charles came running and yelling. Before Roger could grab a piece of wood and start for the bear, Charles was across the swampy ground. "He's mine! I got here first!" he shouted.

"Get away from there!" Roger bellowed.

Charles started to put his hand on the bear's head. Now he stopped, bent over, for a second, and looked at his father, coming toward him with great leaps.

With Charles in this position, the bear made its dying effort. It brought one forepaw up and across Charles' body. The boy screamed and fell. The bear snapped at him and tried to roll over, but Roger got there and beat the bear's head into mush with the piece of cordwood.

He turned back. Anne had picked Charles up in her

arms. Her face was pale. She looked mutely at Roger, a white line around her mouth.

Roger went cold. At least a foot of the boy's intestines was protruding from his abdomen.

For a moment a terrible paralysis seemed to hold him. In all their years on the Trace, this was the thing he had dreaded most—an accident to one of the children.

He started to touch the boy. Then he got control of himself. "Bring him to the fire!" he said in a voice that seemed to come from some other world.

Anne sat down on the wood with Charles in her lap, while Roger got half a bucket of cold water and dipped up enough hot water to make it warm.

"Pour it over my hands," he ordered Liz.

She obeyed; her arms were trembling.

Roger went back and knelt on the ground. The gash was a huge one. At each visible end of the intestine he spread his long fingers as far as possible and began to work the organ back into the boy's body.

Blood ran steadily down Charles' sides and dripped onto Anne's dress, and presently the wood beneath her was wet and red.

When he had it back in place, Roger, holding it there, said to Jeff, "Give me a couple of long strips out of your hunting shirt."

Jeff was slow. Liz pulled the shirt over his head and tore it down the middle. She gave Roger a long strip.

"Anne!" he said.

She held the strip of buckskin tightly against Charles' abdomen while Roger removed his hands.

Roger held the ends down and passed them beneath the body. He tied the ends and took another strip and did the same, having to work a small portion back in place with two fingers.

Virgil Coates came back from looking at the bear. "He should of hibernated by now," he said slowly.

Roger took the boy out of Anne's arms. "Stay here and tend the salt," he told Liz. "We'll call you if you're needed."

He began the long walk back to the cabin. Charles must have been unconscious. Now he opened his eyes and said, "We'll have bear paws for supper." Then he closed them again and lay limp in Roger's arms.

Anne stumbled along behind him in her blood-soaked dress. The sun was well up over the forest. A covey of quail, feeding out of the brush, thundered up at their feet, but Roger hardly heard them.

Marie came to meet them, ash-faced. They laid him in his pine needle bed, and Anne asked, "What can we do, Roger?"

He looked down at her and swallowed. It was the first time he'd ever seen Anne helpless. "Wait and hope," he said, and touched the back of her hand.

"One of us could go to Nashville for a doctor."

"I doubt it will do any good. He'll be well or gone by the time a doctor could get here. But we'll try. Marie!"

"Yas, suh!"

"Tell Gene to saddle the chestnut and go to Nashville without stopping."

"Yas, suh."

"I'll give him a note." He wrote it out on a piece of brown paper. "Gene is a good rider and not as heavy as I am. And no outlaw will bother him except for the horse."

"I think it is the best way," Anne said quietly. "You must be here, if—"

He bowed his head.

Coates and Liz came in at dinnertime. Coates had skinned the bear and cut off its paws; they were a great delicacy. Anne gave the hide to Marie to take care of, and set the paws in the edge of the fireplace to roast.

"How is he?" asked Coates.

Roger shook his head. "He's still bleeding."

They put hot cloths on over the bandages, but toward sundown he was feverish.

"I'll stay tonight and sit with him," said Coates.

Roger nodded, his lips tight. He'd sat with neighbors before, but in all the long years they'd been awfully lucky; the only time anybody had sat with them was when the children had been born—and not always then. He remembered when Charles was born. Anne had been working in the deadening with him and had gone to the cabin for a rest; the next thing he knew he'd heard Marie's buffalo horn, had looked at the sun and had seen it wasn't dinnertime, and then had run back to the cabin to see their second boy, when they'd been expecting another girl. But Charles had made his own place in the family. Where Jeff was slow but kept his thoughts to himself,

76

Charles was quick and vital and never concealed.

Roger had a cupful of whisky and gave one to Coates. He noticed the man drank it and set his cup down quietly.

"The bear paws are done," said Liz.

Roger looked at Charles. He was either asleep or unconscious. "Throw them out," he said harshly.

By morning Charles' fever was up; his heartbeat was fast, but weak. His abdomen was fiery red.

Roger said, "Give him soup if he comes to."

"It isn't gangrene, is it," asked Anne.

He looked down at her gently. "No, it won't gangrene—but it may turn into inflammation that we cannot stop."

He went out to the salt lick for a while, then came back in. The bleeding had stopped, but the boy's face was white.

"It's inside now," he told them at noon. "There's nothing we can do."

They cooled the fever with cloths wrung out in cold water, but it helped very little. Charles woke up once and said he had a stomach ache. They offered him food but he wouldn't eat. Roger shook his head, "When he won't eat, he's mighty sick."

Toward sundown he went back to the salt lick. Coates and Liz and Jeff were working hard. Liz was as good a salt-maker as her mother, and there were nearly four bushels of fine white salt in the wicker baskets lined with buckskin.

"You'd better stop for tonight," said Roger.

"How is he?" asked Liz. Her eyes were red.

Roger shook his head. Suddenly he didn't see too well. "Bile is coming out from under the bandages," he said. "That means his gall bladder is cut open." He blew his nose harshly.

Charles died that night. He had lost so much color and weight that he hardly seemed to be the same boy. When he knew it was over, Roger sat for a while in a stupor. Finally Anne touched him and said, "We've got the others yet."

"Yes." Roger got up and went for Marie to fix up the body.

They buried him at noon, up on the ridge that marked the edge of the deadening. Coates cut out a hollow log for a coffin, and they covered it with clapboards. They stood for a while, nobody talking. Liz cried steadily, softly. Anne's lips were compressed against each other. Coates had a hand on Liz's shoulder. It was late in December, and a cold wind from the northwest blew tiny rivulets of dirt down into the grave from the pile of clods.

Roger looked back toward what was left of the bear's carcass; the buzzards had picked it dry.

"It's no use to blame the bear," he said aloud. "He acted like he was supposed to act. If I was a bear, I'd do the same. Amen."

Coates began to shovel in dirt. Anne and Liz wept. Marie chanted something in a strange and mournful tongue. Voodoo, probably, Roger thought vaguely.

When it was all over, they went back. Coates stayed

to build a graveshed over the grave—a row of logs covered with shakes to keep out animals or vandals.

The doctor from Nashville came two days later with John Swaney. He shook his head. "Mighty afraid of that," he said, "when your boy told me what had happened. Animals' claws have filth on them, and it makes inflammation, and there's nothing anybody can do about it. I trust he died peaceful."

Roger nodded. He got the demijohn and gave the doctor a drink, and then Swaney. Coates shook his head. Roger had a big one. All he wanted was to go under and forget everything, forget the bear and the boy and the grave up on the hill. But life went on. It had to go on. Those who died, died. Those who lived, went on. His strong fingers found Anne's. "We've still got five," he said. "I guess we could afford to give up one. It's better than lots of people who lose them all to Indians or smallpox or yellow fever."

She seemed huddled and cold. Her eyes, looking up at him, were filled with pain. Her face was drawn.

"By the way," said the doctor, "wasn't it you had a brush with the Harpes?"

"I never had trouble with them," said Roger.

"Didn't you have some horses stolen by them?"

"Yes—but I got them back."

"Well, it seems as how they are diggin' up more crimes to lay to the Harpes, and there's all kinds of sarsafari goin' on up at Danville. But that isn't what I meant to tell you." He leaned over. "Little Harpe told somebody that you would vouch for him."

79

"How could I? I never saw him but once in my life."

"That's what I said. And why should you anyway?"

Yes, why should he? Was that a threat by Harpe, intended to reach his ears?

Swaney went on toward Natchez with his half bushel of corn and his overcoat and blanket and his pouch of mail and his tin horn. The doctor stayed that night, and slept in the loft. Roger was a long time going to sleep. Little Harpe had used his name. Was his service with Tarleton going to follow him down here and catch up with him at last? He got up about midnight and looked out toward the ridge. It was a clear and frosty night, and the moon was coming up through the gaunt persimmon trees. He closed the door and went back to bed. Anne put her hand on his chest to soothe him, and he knew she had not been asleep either.

But he had an additional reason for worry that Anne didn't know about. He thought, if justice took its way, the Harpes would both be hanged as soon as a court trial could be held, and then there would be only Hughes to worry about.

6 Virgil Coates was up the Trace pretty often after that—which was only natural, considering. He found a bee tree, and he and Liz and Jeff went off into the forest for most of a day and came back with several gallons of "long sweetening" and ten pounds of beeswax on a packhorse.

Roger knew it was serious when Liz asked if he would get her some store-bought shoes. He took her to Nashville with him, and it was there that he heard the first news of the man who had tried to stab him in the night. He was buying a piece of striped cotton that he knew Anne would like, and half a bolt of jean cloth for shirts and breeches for the younger children. He was wondering how much to get, for it was only a question of time until Liz would need a wedding dress, when a teamster left his four-mule team in the middle of the street and came in for two carrots of Virginia tobacco.

"Where you from?" asked the storekeeper, whose name was Clark.

"Freighting out of the Falls. Brought down some whisky and six barrels of flour from Pittsburgh. These here flatboats are running pretty frequent."

"Still got the flour?"

"Yes. Got rid of the whisky up the road a piece at Hughes' Grog Shop."

Roger asked sharply, "Hughes?"

The man looked up. He was a short man with a

small gray beard on his chin, but he looked able to take care of himself.

"That's what they call him. Sort of a biggish man—sullen like."

"How about the flour? Want to sell it?" asked Clark.

"That's what I brung it down here for."

"How much?"

"I figger about seven pesos a barrel, laid in your front door."

"That's high."

"Worth a man's life, with all the killin's goin' on up in Kentucky."

Roger grinned at Clark. "What do you care? You'll double it to the customer anyway."

Clark shrugged. "Never know when there might be competition. I do my best to hold prices down."

"Give me a hand to roll 'em in?"

"Sure."

Roger looked at Clark. "You're not used to that kind of work. I'll help."

"I'll be obliged," said Clark. "I do get tol'able rusty waitin' on counter all day."

"What do you hear of the Harpes?" Roger asked the teamster.

"You mean them Bloody Harpes?"

"Is that what they're calling them now?"

"That's one of the nicest things they're callin' 'em. Some say they killed eight people in less'n a month up along the Wilderness Road, but nobody checked up on 'em till they arrested 'em for Langford's killing, and they've been digging up bodies ever since. One old man was a peddler, and they split his skull with a tomahawk, and there was two fellers from Maryland—maybe others. Who knows, with bloody murderers like them runnin' loose, I say the Lord should rise up in His wrath and smite 'em dead—and if He don't, we should."

"The Lord has been a little backward about entering the West," Clark observed, lifting one corner of his dirty white apron to make change from a wallet in his pocket.

"These here two men are in jail at Danville with three wives," the teamster said, biting off a chew. "How do you figure that? And all three expectin' babies!"

"The people of Kentucky can do what they like, but I promise you one thing: us here in the Southwest Territory will make it mighty unhealthy for the Harpes or any like 'em," Clark said. "We've got Regulators, with men like Adams here, who will take care of them."

The teamster took a shrewd look at Roger and nodded. Then he stowed away the tobacco in the wallet formed by the overlapping of his shirt. "Regulators is all right, but what we really need is law. When every man has got to stand up and show where he's from and what his business is, then we can clean out these outlaws."

Roger turned to look at Liz. She was trying on the soft, heelless slippers with ribbon to tie them across the foot, her scrubbed face as bright as a dollar. She looked up shyly at him, and he smiled. What else could you do with a girl when a man was setting to her? Anyway, she was fourteen now and old enough to run her own house. He turned back to the teamster. "How far up is Hughes' place?"

"Ten-eleven miles. But you don't have no business up there. It's a wild bunch."

"This man Hughes brought a peck of trouble with him," said Clark. "Some think he's handling stolen goods. There's talk of getting the Regulators after him."

"Regulators?" Roger repeated.

"There's talk he's an ex-Britisher, deserted from the army."

"That's not against him," said Roger. "There are a good many ex-Britishers in the West."

"It's against him if he hides it," Clark said scornfully.

"Maybe he's trying to forget it."

"And maybe," the teamster retorted, "he's a British spy. The country's full of 'em. Everybody knows the British haven't given up the Western Country yet."

Roger took a deep breath. He said, "I'll give you a lift with the flour," and followed the teamster into the street. The man wheeled his mules and pulled up in front of the store. He rolled a hogshead to the back of the wagon. "Got your end?"

"Don't worry about me," said Roger. "Get your end."

The teamster jumped down cackling. "These young

84

fellers all alike. Allus worryin' about the other man's end. I can outlift any two of 'em."

"Like to bet?" asked Roger.

The teamster looked at him through narrowed eyes. "I'll lay you ten dollars even you can't lift with me."

Clark had come outside, and a crowd began to gather. Roger, still holding to one side of the hogshead, said, "Clark, put up ten dollars for me."

Clark said dubiously, "I heard about this feller. He's been makin' more money liftin' than he has freightin'."

Roger smiled. "Has he?"

He saw the teamster put two gold coins in Clark's hand. Then he said. "Give me room through the door," and the crowd opened a lane.

The teamster looked at him suspiciously. "What air you fixin' to do?"

"I'm about to win ten dollars from you," Roger said, pleasantly. He got his hands on the bottom rim of the barrel, pulled it out along the wagon-bed, lifted it onto his stomach, and started for the door.

There was a dead silence. He went through the door sidewise, walked heavily to the counter, lifted the hogshead and set it on the boards.

The crowd cheered. The teamster's mouth was open. Finally he said, "You keep the money, mister. Any man can heave three hundred pounds of flour is entitled to it. I lifted a heap in my time, but I ain't breakin' my back to beat that."

Roger slapped him on the back. "Buy you a drink," he said. Over his shoulder he said to Clark, "Tell Liz

I'll be back in a little while. Tell her to pick out a new dress."

They had a couple of drinks. Then they unloaded the rest of the flour, and Roger declined the offer of another drink. "Daughter's with me," he said. "See you next time."

The teamster nodded.

Liz had picked out some brown woolen material. "Enough for mother and me too," she said, and Roger nodded.

They had supper next door. For twenty-five cents it was "cornbread and common doings," which latter were pork and bacon, but Roger said they could afford to celebrate, and for forty cents they had wheat bread and chicken fixings, which included fried chicken, steak, ham, sausage, and veal. They ended up with real coffee, and Liz was delighted. "Though it's no better a meal than we have at home," she insisted.

Coates was set for a logrolling by the time they got back. He had cleared about fifteen acres, and there were trees three and four feet in diameter on the ground. He had been niggering off these for a week or more—cutting a notch every ten feet or so and building a fire in it, keeping the fire going day and night until the log was burned through. This saved an inordinate amount of axwork on a big tree.

The next morning at sunup they left for Coates' place. The word had been passed up and down the Trace, and twenty-five or thirty families had gathered. It was astonishing, Roger thought, where they all came from. You could ride the Trace for days and swear there wasn't a soul on it but Indians, but let logrolling time come along, or let a family get in trouble from fire, and people came from everywhere.

Coates had a couple of demijohns of whisky and plenty of gourd dippers, and they started work as soon as they got there. The women worked, clearing the brush; the men carried the sections of log to a pile at the edge of the clearing. This was done with five-foot dogwood sticks called handspikes, as big around in the center as a man's arm but slimmed down at each end with a draw-knife. They pried up the log or dug under it and placed the handspikes. A man grasped each handhold, one said, "Up we go!" and they lifted all together. Sometimes it was so heavy they would have to stand for a minute or two, getting their balance. Then they would carry the log to the pile, and finally drag the treetop over the pile.

In the meantime some of the women were fixing dinner in a big iron kettle. Never mind that it was used to wash clothes or to boil salt or to make soap. Coates had a deer hanging from a tree, and the women cut this up and added a wild turkey and a dozen squirrels that some had brought, along with a peck of potatoes and some pickled cucumbers.

There were two teams. Roger was on one; Coates was on the other. They were pretty sober at the start, but as the sun got up and the whisky began to circulate and the sweat started rolling, they began to play pranks. Roger said nothing when he saw Coates' partner dip Coates' end of the stick into fresh cow manure and put it back in place, then holler for Coates to come quick.

Coates bent down to pick up his end of the handspike. He straightened his back, struggling to keep the stick from slipping out of his fingers. The men roared and the women giggled. Coates' face turned red. They dumped the log on the pile, and Roger followed Coates to the creek. "Washin' up early," he suggested.

Coates looked a little crestfallen. "I got the dirty end of the stick," he admitted.

Roger was satisfied then. After supper they had wrestling and racing and log-lifting and tree-climbing and hand-stands, and at all this Roger stood back in his mind and watched, for at thirty-four he was about to lose his daughter to another man. It made him a little sad and it made him feel a little old—and he was a little glad too. So after they were through playing, and when the demijohns were empty and the weathered-faced men and women sat around the fire getting ready to go home, while the children ran and chased each other and played Injun in the dark, Roger got up and told them his secret— which he was sure by now was no secret to any of them. "A week from tonight," he said, "we'll have a house-raising on this place. Mr. Coates is marrying my daughter Liz, and I reckon they'll need a house to raise their young'uns."

The women went "Ooh!" and "Aah!" and the men gave raucous shouts and pounded Coates on the back until he could hardly stand. Liz was burying her face in her mother's lap, and Anne was just looking proud.

So they came, every man with an axe or a grubbing hoe, and Coates organized them into teams. Some notched logs; others heaved them into place. Coates knew his business, all right. The cabin was sixteen by twenty, with a small window on each end, a fireplace in the middle of the north side, and the door in the south.

They laid a puncheon floor, and Coates had some precious nails that he had wrought out of square nail stock, and they put together a massive door with the latch on the inside and a deerskin latchstring running through a hole above it. The latchstring would nearly always be out unless there was an Indian scare.

They selected two young forked trees to hold the ridge pole, and from that they laid smaller poles down the sides and then cross poles, and covered these with shakes that others split out of three-foot pieces of log. Then they laid on logs of small diameter to hold the roof in place.

All this took two days. In the meantime the families camped out in the clearing. When they were all through, Roger invited them to the wedding.

This was held at the Adams' place. There was no preacher in the territory, so Roger stood up before Liz in her new dress and shoes and Coates in a new fancy white linen hunting shirt, that he had bought in Natchez, and Roger said, "Do you take Liz for your wife?"

Solemnly Coates said, "Yes."

Roger said, "Liz, do you take this man for your husband?"

Liz whispered, "Yes, I do."

They danced all night, and emptied three demijohns of rye, and old man Kuykendall from down on the Trace sawed away at his real fiddle, and nobody went home till sunup.

That night Anne said, with her tears wet on Roger's shoulder, "I'm happy for her, Roger, but it's hard too. She's so young. She doesn't know anything."

Roger said confidently, "She'll learn. We all do that. You weren't over six months older."

"I hope he'll be good to her."

Roger took a deep breath. "He'll be," he said confidently.

"One thing I wish, Rog"—she hadn't called him that in a long time—"I wish a preacher would come by so we could make it a Bible wedding."

"There'll be one some day."

She sobbed softly. "And a funeral," she said. "We still owe Charles a funeral."

"Yes. A funeral too. These things all come if we are patient."

The families up and down the Trace were busy then with their own logrollings—for every family tried to clear off a few acres each year, and the Muellers who had come from western Pennsylvania were burned out one night and they had a house-raising for them, so the house-warming for Liz and Virgil wasn't held for over a month. Then the neighbors gathered, each with a gift: gourd buckets, knitted mittens, powder horns, tinder box, a wooden pail, a coil of manila rope from New Orleans. As always, there was rye whisky and fiddling and dancing which was expected to last all night.

But near midnight Roger, dancing as Anne's partner to *Sugar in the Gourd,* heard a strange sound. He stopped for an instant. "That sounds like Swaney's horn!" He went outside. A few minutes later Swaney trotted his horse into the clearing in the moonlight.

"What happened to you?" asked Roger "You're supposed to be on toward the Chickasaw Agency."

"Lame horse," said Swaney. "Slowed me down. I stopped at your place and borrowed your chestnut. I'll pick up mine on the way back from Natchez."

"Sure," said Roger, "but why did you toot your horn? You didn't have to stop to tell me that."

"I come to warn you."

By this time Swaney, on the chestnut, was at the open door of the cabin. He leaned down and looked inside. "A heap of doin's, looks like."

"Yes," said Roger.

"Well, like I said, there's trouble up by Nashville. A man name of Hughes runs a grog shop up there."

"I heard about it."

By now everybody, man and woman, was at the door or trying to get there, listening to Swaney.

"Hughes had a rowdy place. Lot of no-goods hanging around. Some people in Nashville suspected him of crooked dealing, but they never proved anything on him, though some tried, and one man got beat up for his pains."

"Yes," said Roger.

"You heard of the Harpes?"

"Sure," said Coates. "The Bloody Harpes?"

"That's what they call 'em. Both Harpes escaped from the Danville jail a week ago and headed south. Hughes was killed two nights ago—tommyhawked, cut all over with a scalping knife—and the Bloody Harpes was seen in Nashville that night. Clark said to warn all Regulators on the Trace. They think the Harpes are headed this way, and they're killin' right and left!"

7 BUT THE HARPES DISAPPEARED. According to Swaney, who came by every ten days, and what word drifted down from Nashville, western Kentucky determined to drive the Harpes to bay. By this time at least four or five murders had been definitely laid at their door. Lynching parties were organized to look for them, but such was the terror inspired by these monsters as they roamed the country killing men, women, and children—sometimes for no good reason at all—that more than once a heavily-armed pursuit party came face to face with Big and Little Harpe in a narrow forest trail—and turned and fled. The Harpes appeared to be senseless killers, but they were by no means senseless. They changed their dress from time to time, and at one point dressed in the black broadcloth of ministers and traveled for some time under the protection of the cloth, apparently skilled in ecclesiastical talk (as much as any were skilled in the Western Country in those days), and certainly able to deliver long prayers that sounded very real to the listeners, and fervent requests to the deity for blessings on the food of which they were about to partake gratuitously.

In April the three "wives" of the two men were acquitted of complicity in the Harpes' crimes—though it was a little hard to see, old man Kuykendall observed, how they could be wives and still be so innocent. Before acquittal they each were delivered of a child at the expense of the state.

"It is hard," said Mr. Clark at Nashville, "to understand how such children, sired by madmen without regard to wedlock, born in prison and raised by murderers, can ever amount to anything."

It was indeed. On April tenth the Bloody Harpes killed the thirteen-year-old son of Colonel Trabue for a sack of flour, cut up his body and threw it into a sinkhole.

In May Governor Garrard of Kentucky offered three-hundred dollars reward for each of the Harpes. Again posses were organized; again the Harpes were seen and recognized, but their pursuers were either deceived or frightened by the very malignity of their scowling countenances.

The Harpes left Tennessee and began a mad rush westward through Kentucky. They killed again and again, sometimes taking clothing, sometimes money, sometimes nothing but bloody knives and tomahawks.

They roamed into the Illinois Country, where they left two or three dead and mutilated bodies around a campfire. It was rumored time and again that they were headed south for the Trace, and armed parties roamed the country around the southern border of Tennessee, but eventually it was discovered they were north at Red Banks or Cave-in-Rock, and then it was said that even the hardened outlaw killers of Cave-in-Rock had driven them away, and the entire state of Kentucky and the Southwestern Territory armed itself and pulled in the latchstring at night, and it was worth a man's life to appear suddenly out of the forest with a rifle in his hands.

It was said the Harpes had joined their women again, and the Western Country held itself tense, waiting for the next blow. Strangely enough, that occurred over the Cumberland Mountains in eastern Kentucky, beyond Knoxville, where Roger Adams had seen them for the only time. They killed another man there and ripped out his intestines as they had those of Johnson, filled him, too, full of rocks and sank him in the Holston River. Then they started north again up the Wilderness Road to the Gap, their women with them, killing almost daily. Every man in the Western Country should have had a description of them by this time, but those who met them seemed oblivious of their identity or too frightened to take a shot at them, while the several parties of seasoned hunters and fighters seemed, by the very audacity of the Harpes, to be constantly looking in the wrong place. Some said the Harpes were stupid, others that they were clever. Perhaps it was a little of both. At any rate, they had a blood-lust that was terrifying in its intensity.

Around the first of August they came upon two families of Triswords, each with father, mother, several children, and a number of slaves. With two renegade Cherokee Indians, the mad Harpes massacred the entire company except for one man, who escaped and went for help. It now appeared certain that the Harpes

were fleeing south toward the Trace, and again the settlers were alerted. But actually the Harpes had fooled
their pursuers and started to work north. They stopped
near the site of one of the first camp meetings of the
Great Revival, and even the Western Country shuddered collectively when it heard that there, only a few
weeks after the camp meeting ended, Big Harpe
became annoyed at one of their three children, swung
it by its feet and burst its head open against a tree, and
then swung the body into the forest as far as his great
strength would hurl it.

Now they were said to be in western Tennessee, and
Roger Adams, as a member of the Regulators,
received word to join a party in Nashville to hunt them
down along with Coates and Kuykendall. This was
brought by John Swaney, again on his way to Natchez.
Roger looked over his rifle and filled his powder-horn.
He ran bullets while Anne parched a gallon of corn and
filled his knapsack with that and some jerked meat. He
took a sack of charcoal and a tin cup. They finished
preparations late that night by the feeble, sputtering
light of a cob lamp—a hollowed-out corncob wrapped
with a length of string dipped in beeswax and resin, so
arranged that the string was pulled up through the cob
from time to time. Roger didn't sleep. He set off up the
Trace in the dark, for there was little chance of losing
the way. The chestnut had traveled it many times,
and the blazes could be seen even in the dark. More-
over, the underbrush on each side was so thick there
was hardly any other way to go.

The Regulators made a circle through western Tennessee without coming onto a trace of the Harpes, and then Clark said he would have to stay in Nashville and take care of his store, while old man Kuykendall said he had corn to harvest.

Adams took Coates aside. "I want you to go back home and look out for Liz and keep an eye on my family."

"Where are you going?"

"North. I've got a hunch the Harpes will strike up there again."

"What if they come south?"

"You'll be there," Roger pointed out.

"There's not much sense of you risking your neck to catch these fellers when they ain't harming us."

"All of the Western Country is in danger when such men are loose," Roger pointed out. "They may strike anywhere—and their success will bring hordes of killers into this country. Down along the Trace we are bound to feel it if they are not stopped. It might be your family or mine that gets tomahawked next." He shook his head. "I can't sit down there and wait for them. I'm going to find them."

To tell the truth, it was something more that drew him. Little Harpe was probably the only man alive who knew the story of Roger's service with Tarleton and his subsequent desertion from both the British and the Americans, and Roger was fired with a terrible curiosity to know what Little Harpe would say. In one way, Roger knew, it might be better to stay away and not remind Little Harpe of what the dead Hughes had said, but over all there was the inescapable fact that these mad dogs had to be brought to justice. Their continued killing was a menace to the West. So far the activity of outlaws along the Trace had been confined to travelers—and there had been too much of that— but a murder lust like this threatened everybody, traveler and settler alike. Travelers did not have to take the Trace. They could go by boat from New Orleans, or they could travel in large companies and be relatively safe, but the settler had no protection for his wife and children when he was working in the forest. Therefore there could be only one decision: the mad Harpes must be stopped before their blood-lust spread.

The fate of the Western Country was at stake. Roger rode north from Nashville.

He traveled the unbroken wilderness until he came to the place of a man named Tompkins near Steuben's Lick. Tompkins invited him to stay for the night, and Roger asked him if he wasn't afraid to live so far out.

"It ain't far," Tompkins said. "Squire McBee's is only half a mile away. Anyhow, the country is full of armed men, and I don't reckon the Harpes would have a chance. I had two ministers here last night, and they was armed to the hilt."

"Ministers?" asked Roger, pausing as he took off the saddle. "Two ministers? What did they look like?"

"One quite big feller, black curly hair, low over his eyes. The other'n shorter but heavy-built, with red hair. Both of 'em sour-lookin' fellers, but they was right nice. Gave me a cupful of gunpowder, for I ain't had none for quite a spell."

"What names did they give?"

"I don't recollect they gave any names, but they was ministers, all right. They wore the cloth and said some almighty prayers."

"Anybody else come by lately?"

"A Major Love come by this mornin', a surveyor, he said."

"Going which way?"

"Northwest, he said, to see Moses Steigal."

"Anybody else?"

"Nobody else. You ast a lot of questions, mister. Which part are you from?"

He said briefly, "Down on the Trace. Roger Adams."

Mrs. Tompkins appeared barefooted in the doorway. "Supper's ready."

Tompkins scratched his head. "Adams? Air you the feller that won ten dollars from Billy Be Damn by carryin' a hogshead of flour into the store at Nashville?"

"Probably."

Tompkins looked at him with some awe. "You're right well-built at that. Not very big in the belly, but wide shoulders. Billy's been tellin' everybody about that."

Roger finished hobbling the chestnut. "Who's Squire McBee?"

"He's the justice in these parts. A right good man. Hates outlaws."

They had roasting ears and ash cake that evening. It

wasn't very fancy, but, as Tompkins said, it was fillin'.

Early in the night Roger heard dogs barking fiercely to the northwest, and Tompkins said, "Squire McBee's, most likely. He keeps a pack of bear dogs, and they'll put up a fuss if a stranger comes around."

Roger, smoking out his cob pipe, asked, "Why would anybody be coming around to Squire McBee's this time of night?"

"It could be they captured these here Harpes. Up past Steigal's is Robertson's Lick, and there's some travel on the trail."

"I don't like it," Roger said, knocking out his pipe. "I don't like it at all."

He went to bed in the loft. There were no windows, but the chinking had been knocked out to provide ventilation, and through a space of two or three inches Roger could view the entire country to the northwest.

He was restless that night. Perhaps it was the certain knowledge that the two Harpes had slept in this very loft the previous night; perhaps it was the ash cake of which he had eaten heartily. At any rate, he woke up a number of times, and each time was impelled to look through the wide crack between the logs.

Early in the morning he saw the fire. At first it was a lightening in the sky; then it was a rosy hue; and finally there were the tips of leaping flames, and he called downstairs, "Tompkins!"

A sleepy answer, "What's the trouble, mister?"

"There's a fire northwest of here."

Tompkins got up, mumbling. Roger went down the

ladder. They watched the fire for a moment. "Must be Steigal's place."

"Don't you think we'd better go over and give him a hand?"

"It might be we should—though there's talk against Steigal. He comes from Knoxville, and some say he helps out the Harpes."

Roger found his chestnut, and Tompkins rode a sway-backed old mare with a tow-sack for a saddle pad. They went north through the forest to McBee's, but found McBee gone and instead there were five other men who said they had come that morning from Robertson's Lick.

"Pyles is my name. John Pyles. We all live in Christian County. We was taking home some salt and we came by this Steigal place and it was burned to the ground, and there was nobody around. We thought we'd better report it."

"That ain't all," said another.

"I'm tellin' this," Pyles said sternly. "We come across two dead men on the trail—one shot in the back of the head, the other with his brains beat out."

"They left the lick just a while before we did."

"It sounds like trouble," said Roger.

"It sounds like the Bloody Harpes to me."

"Where'd McBee go?"

"He went after Bill Grisson."

"Let's get up there," Roger said to Tompkins.

They came out in the clearing as McBee and Grisson entered it from the other side. "I couldn't come up here alone," McBee said. "The Harpes have been after me for some time."

Roger looked at the cabin site, now reduced to ashes, with a few small columns of smoke still wavering up into the early-morning air. "It's strange," he observed, "there's no one around. Wasn't anybody home?"

"Steigal left yesterday on business," McBee said with narrowed eyes, "but his wife and baby were here as far as I know."

"And what about the major feller?" asked Tompkins.

McBee looked at him and nodded slowly. "He said he was goin' to Steigal's."

Roger rode to the windward side of the ashes. "There's something burned in there besides wood," he said.

They went around and sniffed. Roger got a piece of dogwood and poked at a mass of ashes. When he looked up his face was drawn.

McBee got down. "Drag it out of there," he ordered.

Grisson and Tompkins got handspikes and worked at whatever was under the ashes. They turned it over and rolled it out onto the hard-packed ground around the cabin. McBee's voice was harsh when he said, "It's Mrs. Steigal. Her face is burned off, but her throat has been cut across with a butcher knife."

Tompkins was staring. Suddenly he threw up. Grisson said thoughtfully, "Where's the kid?"

McBee looked at him. "Alongside the mother, most likely."

They dug some more. It was a small child, but its throat was cut also. That much they could tell.

McBee groaned. "This is a bloody night's work."

"You aren't through," Roger said harshly. "There's another body on the other side."

McBee frowned. "Steigal?"

"Steigal wasn't home," Grisson reminded him.

"It could of been the major," said Tompkins.

They rolled that body out. McBee's face was bleak. "It's Major Love. His head was chopped open with an axe."

"We've got to organize a posse," McBee said. "We'll root the Harpes out of the Western Country once and for all. We'll wipe 'em off the face of the earth."

They started back. "We better take the short cut," said Grisson. "They may be waitin' for you, Squire."

McBee nodded. "We've got to get more men," he said grimly. "More men and more arms. These here Harpes ain't ordinary men. They're fiends, and it'll take everything we've got to run 'em down!"

Indeed it would, Roger thought. They were fiends because they struck without warning and without purpose. They killed for gold or they killed for lust. There was no telling where they would strike. Why had they burned this house with three murdered persons in it? To hide the crime? No, he thought not. Sometimes the mad Harpes hid their bodies; sometimes they left them in the open. This was the crux of their insensate madness: they killed because they liked to kill.

They dismounted at McBee's place. Tompkins turned to Roger and asked, "Why are you in this, Adams?"

Now that it was put up to him Roger wasn't sure. Was it to hear what Little Harpe would say, or was it to wipe out the Harpes for fear Jeff would try to follow their example?

Somebody whispered, "Steigal!" and all turned to watch him coming down the trail.

A crease appeared between Steigal's eyebrows when he saw them watching him. His eyes darted from one to another. He dismounted in front of McBee and said, "Why are you lookin' like that?"

"There's been trouble, Moses."

The man's shoulders hunched as if he had been struck a mighty blow. "What kind of trouble?"

"Your house was burned last night."

"My house—" He looked at McBee and whispered, "My wife?"

McBee drew a tired breath. "She was in it."

Steigal fell on his knees. "You're lyin'. You ain't tellin' me true! It's a lie, ain't it?"

McBee shook his head. He put a hand on Moses' shoulder, and looked at Grisson and gave a quick nod toward the house.

Grisson went inside. McBee raised Steigal to his feet, Roger helped him.

"What about the kid?" asked Steigal. "Him too?"

McBee nodded.

Tears were pouring down Steigal's weathered face.

"The Harpes!" he said in a low voice. "The killing sons-of-bitches!"

Grisson came back with a gourd half full of whisky. Steigal drank it like water. "We knew them in Knoxville," he said, "and I told her never to cross them and not to tell anybody who they were. It was the only way I could make it safe for her when I was gone. And now look what they done!"

McBee said sternly, "You've been accused of harboring them."

"I never done it. I hate the Harpes! I only told her that so they wouldn't hurt her—and now they did it anyway!"

"We're gettin' up a posse," McBee said. "You want in?"

The whisky was taking effect. "You damn' right I want in. I'll cut off both their heads and nail them on a post!"

"The first thing is to catch 'em. Nobody ever knows where they'll be next. Where you least expect 'em, likely. They may be headin' south for the Trace."

Roger felt a chill, but he conquered it.

"I'll go up to Robertson's Lick and get some volunteers," Steigal said.

"You still in this?" Tompkins asked Roger.

"I'm in it."

Steigal mounted his horse. Mrs. McBee appeared in the door of the cabin. "You better set an' eat a bite," she said to Steigal. "You can't run around all over the country without food."

"How do you know," Roger asked, "that the Harpes are not staying right in this area?"

"We don't," said McBee. "They tried to get to my cabin last night but the dogs run 'em off. They may try again—or they may go to Tompkins' place—or Grisson's."

"I've got grown boys at my place," said Grisson.

Tompkins was wide-eyed. He shifted his bare feet in the dirt. "I better be headin' back. I'll tell my woman not to be lettin' in *nobody.*"

"Bring her up here," McBee suggested.

"There's too many younguns—but I've got a couple of dogs and an old mule that can smell polecat ten miles off. She's better than a dozen dogs."

"Remember this," said McBee. "Once the Harpes know we're hunting them, we've got to find them. They'll be after us the way they were after me last night—and if we don't get them, they'll be hard to stop."

"They're hard already," said Roger as Tompkins lit off down the road.

McBee nodded. He went in and got a gourd full of whisky. "Sure they are. They may be watchin' us this very minute. They may be headin' north or south or back to Knoxville. Wet your whistle."

"One thing I *never* liked about the Harpes," McBee said.

"What's that?"

McBee took a deep drink. "I fit through the Revolution," he said. "I fit through the Indian Wars and I was at King's Mountain—and I never yet seen a damn' Tory that I would trust. Maybe it's just happen so, but these Harpes was Tories back in Carolina when I was fightin' under Nathaniel Greene." He took another drink and looked up sharply at Roger. "Where you from, Adams?"

"On the Trace, a little south of Nashville."

"Any relation to the Adamses in Massachusetts?"

"Not that I know of."

"There was a man fer you," McBee went on, "Samuel Adams. Could stir up more wars in a few months than an ordinary man could in a dozen lifetimes. Hadn't been for him, there wouldn't of been a Revolution, and we'd still be payin' taxes to the king, instead of which we're fightin' his bloody Tories." He spat. "Tories I don't like, no matter how they come."

8 STEIGAL CAME BACK THE NEXT MORNING with John Leiper, Matthew Christian, and Neville Lindsay from Robertson's Lick. They had stopped to bury Steigal's wife and child and Major Love. Tompkins came in from his cabin, bringing his wife and children. The women parched corn and made journey cake. The men saw to their powder horns and ran a few bullets. Grisson brought his family down to McBee's for safety. McBee had an old Negro servant, and these all fortified themselves in McBee's house with all the firearms the men didn't take, and with orders not to leave, even if they saw their own houses burning.

The posse left about noon, after discussing which way to go. "They might go any direction," McBee said again, "but my guess is they'll head back toward Red Banks. I say let's take a chance and try to pick up sign toward Robertson's Lick."

"All right with me," said Steigal bitterly, "just so I get to cut their heads off with my own knife."

"We found Gillmore's body on the trail comin' this way," said Christian. "From the looks, the Harpes were expecting you, McBee. They must of set the fire to draw your attention."

"I didn't see it," said McBee. "I slept on the other side of the cabin."

"Gillmore's face was cut up somethin' terrible," said

Christian. "The Harpes must have some of them devil's claws."

Roger frowned. "What are devil's claws?"

"Sharp steal hooks that fit on their fingers. A man can take off the whole side of a feller's face with them."

They circled south of the Lick road, and it was not long before they picked up the trail. Most of them were elated. These were all experienced woodsmen, and the trail was as plain as if a wagon had gone through.

"They've got their wimmen and kids with them," said Bill Grisson. "That'll slow 'em down. And they're headin' for the Lick. I say, keep your powder dry."

"Look out for anything," advised McBee. "Everyone in this posse is a marked man. By now they know we're after them. You can't never tell what the Harpes will do next, but there's one thing for sure: they're vindictive as Injuns; they never forget anybody who makes a move against them."

Steigal said bitterly, "They only forget them who try to be friendly."

"They don't recognize friendship. They ain't human, I tell you. There's only one thing for sure, and I say it again: we've got to get them this time or live in fear until they get us."

They jogged along for a few miles, and reached a place where the ground was badly trampled. Roger and Grisson looked it over. "They rode into a herd of buffalo," he reported, "and stampeded them to cover up their tracks. We better separate in pairs and go around the edge. I think we'll pick up the trail again."

They picked up two trails, and followed both. Presently the two came back together. Bill Grisson felt good. "Like I said, they got too big a party. Long as they keep the wimmen with them they won't be able to hide their trail."

"They may cut off from the wimmen," said McBee sourly. "Don't count on anything."

They camped that night on the west side of Pond River, ate parched corn and jerked beef to avoid building a fire, and slept uneasily. "I don't figure they will attack eight armed men," said McBee. "But watch sharp."

There was a sharp gust of rain that night, to help keep them awake. "It'll dim the trail," McBee noted, huddling in his blanket under an oak tree, "but we can't be too far behind."

It was still dark when they started out, and the trail was clear as soon as it became light. An hour after sunup they came across two dead dogs, and Lindsay exclaimed, "Them are Gillmore's and Hutchins' dogs!"

McBee studied the carcasses. "They took the dogs," he figured. "Then they got scared the dogs would bark and give them away."

Roger studied the carcasses too. "It's August," he noted, "and the sun is hot—but the dogs aren't swelled up. They must have done it this morning."

Bill Grisson looked ahead at the forest, perhaps a little fearfully. "They ain't far," he said.

"Keep your voice down," ordered McBee. "Draw up close. You four—Leiper, Steigal, Christian, and Lindsay—follow up on foot, to keep from making so much noise. We'll stay a couple hundred yards behind and lead your horses." But after another mile he drew them back, for it seemed evident the Harpes were keeping ahead of the scouts.

"It's a tarnal shame," Steigal muttered, testing the edge of his knife.

"Hold on!" said McBee. "Look yonder—on the hill."

Steigal exclaimed, "They ain't half a mile away!"

"They're both on foot. Both have rifles."

"There's a third man," said Tompkins, "afoot."

"Follow me," said McBee, "across the meadow!"

They charged out of the trees at a hard gallop. Steigal shouted, "Big Harpe is gettin' away!"

They did look like the two he had seen that night in Hughes' Groggery, Roger thought. Both dark and scowling.

Big Harpe had vaulted into the saddle of his horse and was galloping off, while Little Harpe ran on foot in another direction, and the third man started running toward the posse. This third man suddenly dodged behind a tree, and McBee fired at him.

Steigal shouted, "Don't shoot! It's George Smith!"

Smith came out from behind the tree, limping.

Tompkins said, "You shot him, Squire!"

"A damn' good shot," muttered Leiper. "Once in the arm and once in the thigh."

"I had two balls in my gun," said McBee, dis-

111

mounting. To Smith he said, "What in hell was you doin' with them guys, and why was you actin' like that?"

Smith groaned and held his thigh. "I was mighty nigh out of my senses. I run into Little Harpe going for water. I knew him right off. He ast questions loud, so his brother would hear. Their camp was just a little ways off, and Big Harpe came, and I thought sure they was going to kill me."

"It's funny they didn't," Christian said suspiciously.

"They was gettin' ready to. They kep' askin' questions about the stations—and then you fellers came in sight, and I ran towards you."

"How bad are you hit?" asked McBee.

"Not too awful bad, I reckon. If you could help me home—"

"As soon as we catch the Harpes," said McBee, "we'll see you home. Until then you better sit down and take it easy. Much bleedin'?"

"Not serious, I reckon. One ball went clean through my arm. The other'n is still in my leg, I guess."

"We'll come back for you," McBee promised, "or send somebody."

Steigal called, "Here's their cave!"

It was a shallow rock cave with only a narrow entrance, and they approached it cautiously.

"Come out of there, Harpes!" called McBee.

No answer.

"There's eight of us. Come out or we'll starve you out!"

McBee's words seemed to roll down the hillside and echo among the rocks. A woman appeared in the entrance. "Little Harpe's wife," muttered Steigal. "The one he married in Knoxville."

"Tell 'em to come out with their hands in the air," ordered McBee. "We're all armed and we ain't foolin'."

The woman said in a slight voice, "There's no one here but me."

"Where are the Harpes?"

"Big Harpe was just here," she answered. "He put his women on horses and left."

"Which way?"

She pointed. "That way."

Steigal said, "Stand aside so we can see in."

Roger, looking down from a high spot, said, "There's nobody in there unless they're flat on their stomach."

Steigal and Grisson rode up cautiously. "They're gone, sure enough!" said Steigal.

They started off at a gallop, but five minutes later Leiper said, "We ain't on no trail."

They rode around, examining the ground for sign. Finally McBee swore. "That damn' woman set us on the wrong track so he could get away."

"What about Little Harpe?" asked Roger.

"Hard to tell. He maybe had a horse in the woods, and he's a long way from here by now."

"Or he might have been watchin' us at the cave," said Steigal.

They rode back. McBee went up to the entrance, and

Sally Harpe met him there, a frail, blonde woman who seemed incredibly out of place. McBee advanced on her with his rifle cocked. "You told us wrong. Now give us a right steer or I'll let daylight through you."

She said calmly, resignedly, as if she had anticipated this moment for a long time, "I told you right. I done all I can."

McBee went inside, then came out. "I arrest you in the name of the law," he said to her. "Mose, git one of them extra horses Big Harpe left."

Steigal brought up a horse. "Now I know you can ride," said McBee to Sally, "and this is a good time for you to show it. You ride with me. You other fellers go on ahead and catch Big Harpe."

They rode off, watching the trail more carefully. McBee was not far behind. Leiper shouted, "There he is on yonder ridge!"

"Stop in the name of the law!" bellowed McBee. "Harpe, I order you to throw down your gun and advance empty-handed."

They were less than a quarter of a mile away. Harpe took one look at the posse; then he jammed his heels into his horse's flanks and galloped to the top of the ridge, bent over. Leiper shot at him, but the range was long and Harpe did not present a big target.

They galloped up to the other women, who sat their horses helplessly, each holding a small child. Steigal said grimly, "We're whittlin' 'em down. Tompkins, you and Lindsay stay with these two wimmen. The rest of us'll go on after him."

Leiper had poured a measure of powder down his rifle, and now he fitted a bullet in the muzzle over a patch of cloth. He tried to draw his ramrod, but it stuck. "That damn' rain!" he said. "The ramrod swelled up and I can't get it out. Tompkins, trade guns with me."

"All right."

Leiper, Christian, Steigal, Grisson, and Adams charged the top of the ridge. Big Harpe was spurring his horse down the draw. Steigal shot without effect. Christian fired and said exultantly, "I got him in the leg."

Adams pulled up his rifle, but Leiper was out in front and in the way. Harpe saw this, and, apparently thinking Leiper's rifle was empty, stopped his horse to renew his priming.

Leiper stopped also. While Harpe was pouring the priming powder, Leiper fired. Adams heard the smack of the bullet into flesh and bone, and saw Harpe double over. He thought the man was going to fall, but he straightened, obviously badly wounded, and aimed his rifle at Leiper. He cocked the hammer and pulled the trigger, but the rifle failed to fire. He rose to full height in his stirrups, his surly face showing great pain, and threw the rifle from him.

Leiper and Christian were close. Harpe brandished his tomahawk and cut about him furiously, at the same time spurring his horse.

"Surrender!" cried Leiper.

Harpe's horse seemed tired now, and Leiper rode on one side, Christian on the other, with Harpe still swinging the tomahawk, but not very effectively. The man's saddle was blood-soaked over the cantle, and blood dripped down.

"Ah'll give up," Big Harpe said finally, gasping for breath, "if you stop your horses."

"All right," said Leiper. "Stop your horse."

Leiper and Christian swung and started to reload their rifles. Then Harpe, who had looked to be almost dead, wheeled his horse and galloped away. Leiper's horse bolted after. Christian threw himself into the saddle and overtook the horse and brought him back. Leiper was running to meet them, and both, without loading, galloped after Big Harpe, following his trail into a thick canebrake. They could no longer see him, but they could hear him, and, with Adams right behind, they caught up with Harpe as he was emerging from the canebrake. His horse was walking, and Harpe was hanging to the saddlehorn, his leggings wet with blood. His tomahawk was gone.

Leiper and Christian pulled him out of the saddle.

"He's dying," said Adams. "Your shot hit him in the backbone."

Leiper said wonderingly, "How can a man stay in the saddle with his backbone smashed?"

"I don't rightly know," said Adams.

The three men with their prisoners came up. They left the women under a pecan tree fifty feet away. Harpe's two wives seemed not much concerned about him. Harpe, now lying helpless, said huskily, "Water! Drink of water!"

Steigal said, "We got nothing to carry water in."

Leiper looked at Harpe. "A dying man gets a last wish." He took off one of Harpe's shoes and went back into the canebrake.

"You're dying," McBee told Harpe, "but we ain't taking no chances. We're going to help you along just to be sure."

Leiper returned with water in the shoe. He held the back of it to Harpe's mouth, and the man drank noisily until it was all gone.

"We'll give you time to make your peace with your maker," McBee said.

Harpe lay back, seemingly unconcerned. The strength was going out of his arms, and he did not answer.

Steigal came forward with a knife in his hand. "You damned murderer, you cut my wife's throat and my kid's throat. I am going to finish the job."

Nobody interfered. This was between man and man. Harpe struggled to his right side, but he could not get up.

Steigal seemed to change his mind and pointed his rifle at Harpe's head, but the outlaw began to weave his head back and forth to spoil Steigal's aim.

There was something uncanny about it. "It's almost as if he refuses to die," Adams said in an awed tone.

"He's refused his last time," McBee said grimly. "This time he dies—and not somebody else."

They watched Steigal try to get a bead on him. It was Steigal's family Harpe had murdered, and he was entitled to the killing. He became livid with fury, and kicked Harpe in the thigh. He pointed the gun again at Harpe, and still the man jerked his head back and forth to evade the shot. Finally Steigal threw down the gun and laughed weirdly. "All right! You don't want me to shoot you, so I won't! But I told you I was going to cut off your head, and I am! Dead or alive, your head is coming off, Harpe."

Leiper said, "Here's Harpe's knife. It's sharper."

Steigal took it and tried the blade. Adams watched through narrowed eyes as Steigal took Harpe by the hair and turned him over, face down. Steigal held him there with one hand while he made a deep incision across the man's neck; Adams could hear the blade scrape on bone. More blood gushed out. Harpe was too weak to move, but he muttered, "You're a god-damed rough butcher, but cut and be damned!"

It didn't stop Steigal. The man was crazy mad, and nobody interfered. He jerked Harpe over on his back and slashed across his neck in front. Then he took hold of Harpe's head and twisted it off. He held it by the curly black hair while the blood drained out of it, and finally held it up triumphantly. "There, thank God, is the last of Micajah Harpe!"

McBee asked presently, "What'll we do with it?"

"Stick it up somewhere as a warning to any who feel like following in his path," said Leiper.

"I say take it to Robertson's Lick," said Steigal.

"It's thirty-five mile."

McBee looked at the sun, "We can easy make it today."

• • •

They stuck the head on the sharpened end of a limb by the side of the crossroads, and no placard was needed. The grim relic was warning enough. They took the three women twenty miles to Red Banks and put them in jail. They went to a saloon and had a drink, and Roger Adams asked the question that had been bothering him, "What about Little Harpe?"

"We scared him plumb to hell an' gone out of the country," said Steigal.

"I wonder about that."

"You got nothing to worry about," said Tompkins. "He don't know you anyway."

"Maybe not," Roger said thoughtfully, and turned to McBee. "Do you think he'll come for the women?"

McBee downed his drink and wiped his whiskery mouth. "Not Harpe. They never worry about their women. No, I figure he'll take up in some new part of the country. Even a Harpe has got sense enough to know that he has wore out his welcome in this state."

Tompkins and Adams started back together. Tompkins was somewhat talkative. "I never seen a feller git so upset as that Steigal."

"You would have been brushed too if it had been your wife and kid."

"I knew her," Tompkins said. "She was one of the most jimberjawed critters I ever seen. Never stopped her tongue day or night."

"There's things between man and wife," Adams said, "that count for more than tongue-wagging."

"Anyway," Tompkins said gleefully, "we're rid of the Harpes. Squire McBee said so." He looked at Adams. "Maybe you'll have comp'ny down on the Trace."

Adams pushed the chestnut into a faster walk. Home seemed very far away.

9 WHEN HE GOT BACK HOME, the leaves of the corn were ready to turn yellow, and all hands went into the field. They had nearly three-hundred acres of corn that year, and there was no time to lose, for it was dry and the leaves would turn fast. They stripped the leaves below the ears, gathered them in bunches, and lodged them in crotches of stalks. After the fodder was pulled, a sled went through the field. They bound each handful of leaves with a leaf, and took them to the feed shed beyond the cook cabin. Then the upper portions of the stalks were cut off, and the ears left on, to be snapped after frost and stored in a rail crib. Later in the winter they'd have some corn-shuckings.

Roger would turn the horses loose to pasture in the cane or feed them on fodder. There was browse to be cut for the cows, so he set Will and Betty to cutting the bark and small branches of pignut, slippery elm, and beech trees.

In these days just before the leaves began to fall to the ground to be dry and crackly underfoot, squirrels were easy to get and made good soup. Roger would walk through a squirrel grove, making a great deal of noise. The squirrels, fat from acorns, walnuts, and pecans, and curious as always, would stay out of sight, following the tree trunk to watch Roger, unaware that Jeff was coming fifty yards behind. Jeff was keen-eyed. He could see a squirrel's tail farther than some people could see a nest, and he had learned to shoot just below the critters so the shattered bark flew out and stunned the animal, dropping it to the ground without a scratch. He followed along behind his father, marked half a dozen squirrels, and then shot the nearest one. From then on it was a matter of their both approaching a tree, one from each side, and either taking the shot when it was offered. Under such stalking it was hard for a squirrel to stay out of sight, for he would stretch himself practically level with the ground to watch one hunter, apparently not aware that its tail would be almost on the opposite side of the tree.

Roger was well-pleased with the results. They were tough critters to skin, those squirrels, but they made a mighty good stew—twenty or thirty cut up in the big iron pot and simmering in the fireplace for hours.

Anne had had a good garden that summer. There were plenty of potatoes, which she buried in a root cellar. She had tried white potatoes, but without much luck. String beans and pumpkins always did well, and they could be dried and hung from the roof. As soon as the corn was hard enough, she rubbed the ears over a piece of tin that had been roughed up on the back side by driving nails through it. This gritting made a tasty cornmeal. Later, when the heads grew harder, she ground them in a hominy block—a hardwood stump with a dish-like place scooped out at the top, and a hardwood pestle to crush the grains. The fine material that resulted was used as flour; the coarse was boiled as hominy grits.

There were also nuts that the smaller children, even Sarah, could gather in the fall. Often they made a party of it, with Gene and Marie and their young'uns too. Persimmons came after the first frost when a tall man could shake the fairly small but straight-trunked trees, and the ripe fruit would drop to the leaf-carpeted ground. There were sweet wild plums to be found in sandy spots, and wild grapes almost anywhere. There were fish to be had in the Tennessee River—channel catfish in particular, and these grew very large and very tasty. The good white meat flaked off of the bones at a touch, and around the edges of the skillet a little cornmeal, fried to a golden brown, was better than a peddler's candy.

"But some day," Anne said wistfully, "I wish we'd plant some wheat so we could have white bread."

"I'll ask for seed next time I'm in Nashville," said Roger. "It all went to stalk at first, but maybe the corn has taken some of the richness out of the ground."

He rode down to Coates' place occasionally, and one day he came home and announced gravely, "Liz is going to have a baby, looks to me."

Anne had a twinkle in her eyes. "How long does it take a man to see things like that?" she asked.

Marie had another baby, but they seldom caused her to miss more than a couple of days' work.

Roger went by himself one day to examine the graveshed up on the ridge. He saw where coyotes had dug around it, but not deep enough to bother. He dropped rocks in the shallow holes to discourage them.

He got Virgil Coates and Kuykendall to go with him on a hunt to get the bear's oil used in cooking, for the Mississippi country was still overloaded with bears. There were two expeditions to kill wild hogs. Up in Kentucky they raised hogs and kept them penned up; down here they had a drive in the fall and killed what they wanted, getting bacon, ham and lard without having to feed the animals. There was also ginseng to be dug in the fall. This could be traded at Nashville for dried friut, lead and powder, apples, white potatoes, and whisky. Also in the fall when the turkeys were fat from acorns, they built turkey traps and baited them with corn. They usually got more than they needed, and took these to Nashville to trade.

With the smaller children beginning to be a help, and with considerable land cleared off, Roger was able to produce more than they could take in trade. He took the big Spanish silver dollars, and sometimes gold pieces, from Clark, and carried them home concealed in a bucket of deer tallow. He cut a hardwood block about a foot long, drilled holes in it big enough for the coins; then he could plug the hole and cut the plug off flush, so the coins could not be taken out without splitting the block, which he kept under the bed.

Jeff spent much of his time trapping coons, the pelts of which were used in place of small coins. The soft Spanish dollars were being cut into quarters and eighths, but the edges of the pie-shaped wedges were sharp and would cut the bottom out of a pocket.

It was almost Christmas when Anne suddenly, without apparent information, got out extra quilts and rode down to Coates' place. Liz had a hard time, and Roger paced the deadening back and forth a good many times, followed by Virgil, shuddering at Liz's screams, until finally Anne came to the door and blew her horn.

They both were running. "What is it?" asked Roger.

"Twins," said Anne proudly. "Boy and a girl."

"No wonder," breathed Roger.

"How's Liz?" asked Virgil.

"Good as can be expected."

Liz was lying back, pale-faced but smiling, a baby on each side of her.

Virgil stared. "Well, I never—"

"These women," said Roger, "always have something up their sleeves."

But Virgil, after a moment on his knees at Liz's side, drug out a demijohn of whisky from under the bed. "Git a gourd," he told Roger. "It's sure time to celebrate. Twins!" He stared at Liz and then at Anne. "Couldn't a man have no warning?"

Anne was rolling down her sleeves. "What do you need warning for? It's a natural thing, isn't it?"

"Well, sure, but—"

"There's nothing to but about," Anne said severely. "You still got your wife, and you've got two nice healthy younsters. I'll send Marie down to help out for a few days," she said, business-like.

"Anything you want?" Roger asked Liz.

She smiled softly. "I have everything now," she said.

Things went along quietly for almost a year. Roger expanded his acreage with the help of two Negroes he bought from Clark. The Great Revival was sweeping the country, and camp meetings were held in eastern Tennessee, but Roger and his family did not go. "We have more important things to do," he said, "than go up there and make public fools of ourselves having the jerks or holy laughter."

"Roger!"

"What else is it?"

Anne was working on a buckskin hunting shirt for Jeff. "There's some people don't think so," she said.

"Those who don t think it are welcome to go," said Roger. "I'm not stopping them."

"Liz hasn't had a Bible wedding yet," Anne reminded him.

He looked at her in the light of the fireplace. "I'll send word by Swaney."

"We'll have to be looking our best."

"What for?" Roger growled.

She straightened, puzzled. "I don't know what's got into you, Roger."

"There's nothing into me. I just don't go along with these camp meetings and I don't see why a preacher is any better than anybody else."

"Roger," she said, "I hope you don't talk that way at the wedding."

He reached for the demijohn under the bed. "I always manage to talk right, don't I?"

"You've had raising," she admitted, and looked up to stare at him. "You've never told me about it."

"About what?"

"Where you were raised."

"Nothing to tell," he said, and emptied the cup.

He went out and walked around the cabin, thinking it over in the night, hearing the bullfrogs boom down in the swamp, an occasional crashing in the canebrake as some large animal pushed through, the distant yapping of a coyote, the rising hum of mosquitoes from damp underbrush. The Negroes were singing their strange, rhythmic songs in the far cabin. Jeff had ridden up the Trace a few miles to spark a girl in a new family come down from Virginia. South on the Trace he heard dogs barking, for there were several families now between his place and Coates'.

Why was he so contaminated edgy lately, anyway?

He went back inside without answering this question. He had another cup of whisky and lay down on the bed. The next thing he knew, Anne was trying to roll him under the covers. "Jeff is back," she said. "He brung a deer that he shot on the way home."

"Kid's a good shot," Roger muttered, and got into the bed.

About midforenoon the next morning the dogs began yapping, and Roger went to call them off. There were five men, sunburned and peeling, dirty as Indians, dressed in filthy canvas shirts and trousers, unshaved for three weeks, and each with a bundle wrapped in an old blanket.

"Where you from?" asked Roger.

The leader, haggard-eyed and emaciated, answered with a Kentucky drawl. "We come up from New Orleans, mister. You got any objection?"

"None at all," said Roger, looking them over. "Go down on a flatboat?"

"That's what we did."

"And walking back home?"

"How else d'ye git there?"

"If you took goods to New Orleans, you could buy horses to ride back."

"Horses!" The man tried to laugh. "We started out whip-sawing—six men, two horses. The damned Spaniards wanted two hundred dollars for a horse, so we thought to beat 'em at it."

"You're only five men and no horses," Roger noted.

"One man got malaria, and we left him with some Indians. One horse got mauled by a Mississippi tiger, and we ate him. The other grazed too close to a swamp, and the alligators pulled him in. It's a hell of a country you got here, mister. The snakes lie in the trail in the daytime, and the mosquitoes and gnats eat us up at night."

Roger said, "You went down of your own free will, didn't you?"

"Sure—and we're comin' back the same way."

"Well," said Roger, "no use fighting over it. You fellers are bushed. Why don't you settle yourselves for a while. We just killed a deer, and there's plenty of grits."

The gaunt-faced man turned to the other four. "What do you say, fellers?"

"I'm tired," said one, "*and* hungry."

"One of you hasn't got shoes," Roger observed.

"Wolves chewed 'em up one night."

"After salt, probably. Anne!" She appeared in the doorway. "Can you cook up that deer ham for five men?"

She said, "If they're not in too big a hurry."

The emaciated one said, "We got plenty of time, ma'am." He watched her turn back inside. Then he came to Roger. "We got no money," he said.

"Money isn't needed. Deer are free, and we've got more corn than we need, this year."

"Glad to hear somebody has got somethin'."

"Did you spend all your money in the swamp?"

"Not all of it." The man dropped his bundle. "We had money startin' back, but somebody knew it. Six men held us up right after we lost our last horse, and took every picayune. That was just north of Natchez."

"Get fed up," said Roger, "and you haven't far to go. Nashville is only two days' ride."

"Take us a week." He went to the creek and washed off some of the dirt. He scrubbed his hands with sand, but they were still filthy.

Roger gave them all a cup of whisky, and they sat in the sun at the front of the house. "I've got some moccasins for you," Roger told the barefooted one. "A man needs something on these rough trails."

"Obliged," the man said. His feet were puffed and swollen.

Roger went inside.

"I don't like their looks," Anne whispered.

"They've had bad luck."

"It's more than that. They probably got run out of Natchez by the authorities."

"Never mind," said Roger. "They're hungry."

"I don't mind feeding them," she said, "but I don't want you to get your throat cut."

She called them in presently, with five big deer steaks in the middle of the table, and a plateful of grits for each one. Roger said. "Maybe they'd like some coffee." He knew Anne didn't approve it, for their coffee supply was low, but she hung a kettle on to boil.

Roger, feeling expansive, glanced at the leader. The man's eyes were fixed on the money blocks under the bed and easily visible from where they sat. The fellow saw Roger watching him and mumbled, "Must be money, farmin' down here."

"It depends," said Roger.

"Depends on what?"

"Some work harder than others."

"Some don't get ahead no matter how hard they work."

Roger was beginning to dislike the fellow, but he maintained his pleasant air until the meal was over and the men had finished their coffee. "Now," he said, "we'll give you all some parched corn and a wallet of jerked meat. If you keep going you can make Colbert's Ferry tonight."

"Maybe we'll stay around a while," the emaciated man said, his burning eyes fixed on Anne.

"This is not a hospitable country at night," Roger answered, still pleasantly.

They left without thanks, and Roger thoughtfully watched them go.

Anne shook her head. "They're bad men," she said. "I don't like the way he looked at your money blocks."

"He can't hurt them by looking,' Roger said mildly.

"Roger, if I hadn't known you so long I'd say you are a fool."

"But you have known me for quite a while," he reminded her, "so be sparing of your judgment."

That evening he said to Jeff, "No sparking tonight. I want you around."

Jeff looked at him but didn't answer. After supper it was dark, and he posted Jeff behind a tree two hundred yards from the front door. "Keep your eyes open," he said.

"Is it Indians again?"

Roger said, "We haven't been bothered by Indians for years. No, it isn't Indians. It may be worse."

Jeff slid away in the darkness. Roger went inside and saw there was a bullet in the barrel of his rifle. He put in fresh priming powder and stepped outside, aware of Anne's eyes on him as she was combing her hair and getting the children to bed.

He squatted down behind the hominy block and waited. There would be no moon. He saw Anne walking back and forth as she picked up clothing and hung it on pegs. She came to the door once and looked out. He did not move. She went back to the fireplace and sat down in the split-bottom chair, her head bent low as she mended a dress for Betty. The window shutters were open, and Roger had a good view of the north side.

The dogs quieted down; the night noises came up. From somewhere far off came the bass voice of an old bull alligator. Roger stayed where he was.

He was low, watching against the stars, and he saw the deeper shadows drift out of the brush and move down toward the cabin. Some went to the window, others to the door. He heard a low word, and Anne's startled exclamation, but he waited. He saw a man start in the window, but a rifle crashed through the night behind him, and the man crumpled and fell. The other shadows wheeled about, then ran to the brush from which they had come. Roger waited. Presently Jeff slipped alongside. "I got him!" he whispered elatedly.

Roger squeezed his shoulder. After a moment he said, "Go up quietly and call to your mother."

The door of one of the Negro cabins had opened for a moment. Marie had looked out, but, seeing no disturbance, had turned back and closed the door.

He heard Jeff call to Anne, and he was proud, for the boy moved like an Indian. He heard Anne's low answer, and her question, and waited a minute more. Anne was a good wife. She had grown up in Kentucky, and rifle shots in the night were not new to her.

Presently Roger went to the cabin. He got the fallen man by the feet and dragged him around to the other side of the cabin where he could not be fired on from the brush. Those five men might have firearms by now.

"Jeff," he said, "bring a light."

He heard Jeff pick a splinter of pitch pine out of the wood box. He lit it in the fireplace, and then came out the front door. He glided around the corner of the house and shielded the light. Roger looked down at the face of the emaciated man. The eyes were no longer burning. Roger felt his wrist. "Bring a rope," he said, "so we can drag him out of the yard."

"What were they after?" Jeff asked when he came back.

"Money—guns—anything, Jeff." They tied the rope around his feet and pulled him across the dirt. "I'm afraid we'll see a lot like this in the next few years. Swaney says flatboats are going downriver by the hundred, and this is the only way most of them can get back home. We'll have to watch sharp from now on."

"He was like an Indian," Jeff said. "You just fed him today, and he came back to rob you."

"No, that isn't Indian. It's smarter to say that's like some men. The color of the skin has little to do with it."

They left the body under the trees. "If the coyotes don't get him tonight, the buzzards will tomorrow," said Roger.

"Maybe we ought to bury him."

"I fed him," said Roger. "Burying him is stretching hospitality."

10 IT WAS NOT UNTIL THE NEXT MORNING that they found the chestnut had been stolen, and Roger sent word to Nashville.

Three days later a rider came into the yard. He rode on a sheepskin over the saddle. He carried saddlebags before and behind, and a blanket with an umbrella strapped up in it. He wore a cloth hat, a coat, jean trousers, and a rough homespun shirt. An overcoat was thrown over his big horse's withers.

The dogs, yapping, surrounded him until Anne went to the door and scolded them. She said, " 'Light, Reverend."

He got down. "Mr. Swaney tells me you have need of my services as a child of the Lord."

She smiled. "Come in and sit, Reverend. We've been needing a minister for a long time."

"I'm at your service, ma'am."

Roger came in from the smokehouse and poured a cup of whisky. "You going on down to Natchez, Reverend?"

"Not I—though there is plenty of need for men of the cloth in that wicked town." He drank half of the whisky.

"It ought to be a good place to set up in business," said Roger, helping himself.

"The Trace is said to be infested with outlaws who do not respect either the Lord or His servants."

"They haven't bothered Swaney."

"Swaney leads a charmed life—and he carries nothing valuable," the preacher said wisely.

Roger said, "Reverend, we need a funeral and a wedding. Can you stay three or four days?"

"Whatever is required," the minister said pompously, "that will I do."

They put the reverend in the loft, and just before they went to sleep Roger said softly to Ann, "He'll preach a good funeral, I think. It took him half an hour to say the blessing."

"I asked him to make it a long one," Anne confessed. "I thought we could make up a little for lost time."

Everybody up and down the Trace came to the funeral. It was held at noon at the grave of Charles. The women had practiced their songs every night, and now they stood on the ridge under the pecan trees and sang lustily.

Anne wept and Roger was solemn, remembering. Liz cried too, while the twins, alarmed at the strange goings-on, began to howl lustily. The dogs barked and it was taken up by others. The minister joined in with sonorous amens, and then he went into his sermon. He extolled the virtues of heaven and threatened them with the dire consequences of hell for two hours, and finally brought them all to tears with a touching tribute to this little lad, whose soul had not had time to become "tainted with avarice, greed, or jealousy—a pure, innocent babe, as helpless and trusting as a shorn lamb, and sent into eternity by a foul blow from a forest brute."

Everybody said it was a good sermon, and some said it was the only one they'd ever heard. After the funeral, and just before the last hymn, the minister announced, "Bring your extra salt to Dunn & Dunn at Nashville, and we will treat you right. Fine cane sugar for sale also at current prices."

The one thing sure about it was that Charles had had a decent Christian burial at last—and it was time to get on with the wedding.

That occurred two days later. Virgil slaughtered a steer for the barbecue, and brought two kegs of whisky down from the Red Heifer Distillery. He and Roger wore shoes and homespun jean pants, with white linen shirts and blue suspenders. They went through the ceremony with Anne holding the twins in her lap, and later she said, "Liz was just as radiant as the night they were married first."

"I reckon Virgil has made her a good husband," said Roger.

Afterward the men drank whisky and the women feasted until midnight, while the younger boys and girls danced on the rough board floor and played kissing games until sunup. Roger found the minister asleep in a corner and took him back to their own cabin. He gave him a gold Spanish quadruple and thanked him for coming when they started him back to Nashville the next day.

"I aim to be on hand from now on," the minister said. "Call on me whenever you need me."

"We'll do that," said Roger.

A few weeks later Swaney brought word that the sheriff in Nashville had found the chestnut and had caught the man who had it; he requested Roger to appear and claim his property.

"They're getting pretty fancy up there, with a sheriff, aren't they?"

"Civilization is on the way," Swaney said. "And high time, too."

"Things are getting pretty well settled, up in Kentucky, I suppose."

"Since you fellows took care of Big Harpe, the outlaws have been pretty scarce."

"That was less than two years ago," Roger noted.

"Yep. Time sure gits. Some day they'll have wagons on the Trace, even."

Anne, preparing the parched corn for Roger's trip to Nashville, asked, "What will they do to the man who took the horse?"

"Usual thing, I suppose."

She shook her head. "I'm getting old, Roger. Those things didn't used to bother me, but I hate to think of it now."

"I never did like it," he said, "and I don't now. But it's still a country of violence. The law-breakers must be treated with violence or the country will go back to the Indians."

While he was saddling a dapple gray that he had bought from another planter, a stranger rode into the yard. Roger called off the dogs and told the stranger to alight.

"I'm workin' for the gover'ment," the man said. "Name of Logan, headquarters at Nashville."

Roger frowned. "What do you want?"

"Takin' the census. A little late gettin' around, but better late than never, hah, hah."

"Ask your questions," Roger said coldly.

"Name?"

"Roger Adams."

Logan wrote the answers on a sheet of paper nailed to a board.

"Are you the head of the family?"

"Yes."

"Wife living?"

"Yes."

"How many children?"

"Two boys, two girls."

"Blacks?"

"Five adults, nine kids."

"Nice place you got here."

"We like it."

"Adams? You any relation to John or Samuel Adams?"

"Not that I know."

"I knew some Adamses in western Pennsylvania."

"Not them, either."

The man kept on with that persistent curiosity that was a part and parcel of the Kentucky frontier. "Where *did* you come from then?"

"I was born in England," Roger said shortly.

"Served in the Revolutionary War, I suppose."

Once more they were trying to ferret out his secret. Finally Roger said, "No."

"Well, no offense. I was just going to say this country in here has been under North Carolina law and never been surveyed. A man with a soldier's land warrant, of course, would be safe enough."

Roger towered over him. "Do you mean there is a danger of losing my land?"

The man backed away hastily. "No, of course not. Only—I just thought—well, there are going to he some laws passed about this land some day, and a man with military scrip would be in good shape, of course."

"I took tomahawk rights on this land in 1783," Roger said, "when there was nobody down here but Indians, and I've been here ever since, raised a crop every year. What better rights do you want than that?"

"No offense, mister. I didn't—"

"And that isn't all," Roger thundered. "I can drive a nail in a tree at sixty yards with my rifle, and my son can drive it through. I serve notice right now, that if anybody wants my land they'll have trouble getting possession."

"All right, mister."

Roger advanced toward him. "I think you're a damned speculator!" he shouted. "If you're out scouting for land, you'll lose your scalp down here. We took this land from the wilderness, and we aren't going to give it up to somebody who wants to buy it for nothing and sell it at a big profit."

The census taker went on down the road.

"What were you shouting at that man for?" asked Anne.

Roger poured himself a cup of whisky and sat down to cool off. "He was snooping. Asking questions about where I came from, trying to find out about my title to this land."

Anne sat down beside him and put her brown hand on his. Her fingers were still soft. "Whatever it is, Roger, you're going to have to tell it some day."

"We can move on," he said glumly.

"With all we've got built up?"

"We aren't old, Anne. I'm only thirty-five."

"We've put in a lifetime of work, Roger. We've got too much to lose."

"That's always the trouble with having," he said. "You're afraid to lose."

"You never told me anything about yourself, Roger, and I never asked you. I took you at your face value—and I've never been sorry. But you've been living with a secret for a long time. Whatever it is, you can't keep it forever. You'd best bring it out into the open and face it." She smiled at him. "I'm sure you never did anything bad, Roger."

"No," he said. "I don't think it was bad—but it could be made to look bad."

"Will anybody try?"

"One man might."

"Where is he?"

"I don't know."

"Then why not tell me about it?"

"There may come a time," he said, "when I'll have to answer—but if that one man dies, I won't. No, I'll wait."

She stared at him. "Roger! You aren't thinking of killing this man!"

He drained the cup. "First time it entered my head," he said. He got up and went out.

He located the sheriff at the public market. "Hear you found my chestnut."

"Clark says it's got your brand," the sheriff said, spattering the far wall with tobacco juice. "So does Swaney."

"Mind if I look?"

"Not at all." The sheriff got up. He carried a knife and a pistol. He led the way to a pen outside. "Look like yourn?"

Roger cleared his throat. The chestnut turned, then trotted over toward him and put its muzzle over the top rail.

The sheriff nodded complacently. "Yourn, all right."

"What's against him?"

"Eight days' board at two bits."

"I'll pay it and take the horse."

"There s one thing." The sheriff chewed his tobacco thoughtfully. "I want you to be a witness at the trial."

"What trial?"

"Trial of the horse thief."

"When will it be?"

"Judge Wilson is holding court now. We'll try this case in the morning."

"I'll be there," said Roger.

Court opened at eight o'clock. Judge Wilson sat behind an ordinary table and tilted his chair back against the wall of the log courthouse, with his feet on the table. "Next case."

A small, bespectacled man got up and read rapidly from a book; "The State of Tennessee versus Andrew Bean."

"Bring in the horse thief," said the judge.

The sheriff brought through the crowded courtroom a man still clad in tattered canvas pants and shirt. He was unshaven and his hair was uncombed. He looked like a wolf Roger had once seen with its leg tendons severed, put into a pit with half a dozen dogs at a wolf-baiting.

"How do you plead?" asked the judge.

The man seemed afraid to say anything. A youngish fellow with red hair and slick clothes got to his feet. "Your honor, he pleads not guilty."

The judge looked a little astonished. "You want a jury?"

"We do."

"You know this feller was caught with the goods on?"

"Your honor," Attorney McClanahan said firmly, "that is a fact yet to be established in this court."

The judge glared at him. "Outside of court," he said, "I know damn' well he's guilty, because I helped catch him."

"If your honor please, we request our constitutional rights be observed."

"All right. Hey, some of you fellers from the back of the room! Come up here and be examined for witnesses."

The jury was chosen within half an hour. The prosecuting attorney, sitting in a split-bottom chair with his feet also on the table, read from a paper; "The defendant, one Andrew Bean, is charged with offending the peace and dignity of the State of Tennessee by stealing one chestnut horse branded RA connected, without the owner's consent, and then and thereby feloniously removing said horse from the owner's premises." He droned on and on. Presently he looked up. "Mr. Adams, will you be sworn?"

The bespectacled clerk administered the oath, "Do you swear to tell the truth, the whole truth, and nothing but the truth, s'help you God?"

"I do," said Roger.

"It ain't legal," the judge said. "He didn't raise his right hand."

McClanahan jumped up. "Your honor, I object to the court's trying this case for the prosecution."

"Objection overruled," the judge said. "And sit down."

"Your honor—"

The judge tilted forward and glared at him. "Do you want to be thrown out of this courtroom?"

"No, your honor, but Blackstone—"

"Blackstone ain't tryin' this case. This man is a horse thief and we're here to convict him."

McClanahan was obviously new in Nashville. "Your

honor, this is not a court of justice. This is a farce."

The judge glared at him. "Fined five dollars for contempt of court," he said, and added to the sheriff. "Make him pay it before he practices any more law in this court."

McClanahan sat down. His mouth was open and his face was red with indignation, but he kept still and paid the fine.

"What kind of money is it?" asked the judge.

"It's good money," snapped McClanahan. "It'll take you from here to sundown."

"First National Bank of Baltimore," said the sheriff slowly, spelling out the words with his lips first.

The judge pocketed the note. "Proceed with the trial."

Roger was sworn in again, but after the brief flurry between court and defense attorney, there was a rising hum of whispering in the courtroom, the occasional spat of tobacco juice, and a hubbub when two dogs ran into the courtroom and staged a fight in the aisle.

Roger testified that the chestnut was his; that it had disappeared on a certain night about a month before; that the prisoner had been at his cabin that day.

"What was he doing there?" asked the prosecutor.

"He had come up the Trace with four other men from New Orleans, and I gave them something to eat."

Murmurs arose from the jury. "That settles it," said one lanky barefooted man who wore a shapeless felt hat. "Any man would steal a man's horse after he's been fed—" He spat at the far wall.

The sheriff testified that he had found the prisoner riding the horse from Nashville, that he had arrested him, that the chestnut had known its owner.

"Gentlemen of the jury," said the judge, "what is your verdict?"

The lanky, barefooted man said, "I think he's guilty, your honor."

"Does the jury agree?"

There was a unanimous nodding of heads. "Sheriff," said the judge, "didn't you confiscate some whisky from a feller who didn't have a license to sell it?"

"Yes, your honor."

"I have an idee," said the judge, "that we could right here and now sample that confiscated goods in preparation for the next trial."

"Yes, your honor." The sheriff went outside and brought hack the demijohn. He handed it to the judge, who took a deep drink and handed it to the prosecuting attorney. After the attorneys came the jury, then the convicted thief.

"Now," said the judge, wiping his lips with the back of his hand, "you got anything to say before I pass sentence?"

"Your honor," McClanahan said softly, "may I say something?"

The judge glared. "To me—not to the jury. They've already given their verdict."

"Your honor, where did this—"

The two dogs chased each other into the cabin and began fighting. Somebody kicked them out.

"Your honor, where did this alleged crime take place?"

"It ain't no *alleged* crime," the judge reminded him. "The jury has found him guilty."

"Then may I ask where this crime took place?"

"Where's your claim?" the judge asked Roger.

"Two days' ride south of Nashville."

"Is that south of the Tennessee state line?"

"Yes."

"Your honor, may I point out that the jurisdiction of this court extends only to the state line."

The judge's chair came down hard on all four legs. He thundered, "What court *does* have jurisdiction over that part of the country?"

McClanahan answered softly, "None that I know of, your honor."

"Then," the judge said complacently, "this court assumes jurisdiction for the purposes of this trial."

"But, your honor, that exceeds the legal bounds—"

The judge sat up straight. "Young man, this court is sworn to uphold the law, and you are an officer of the court and you are sworn to uphold the law."

"But—"

The judge glared triumphantly. "Fined five dollars for obstructing justice," he declared. "And be more respectful or you may find yourself barred from practicing in Nashville. This court," he went on, "sits for the administration of justice, and we aren't letting no horse thief loose on a technicality. Prisoner at the bar," he said sternly, "You have anything to say for yourself?"

The man was now terrified, and Roger felt sorry for him. "No, your honor. Yes, I—no—"

"Make up your mind!" the judge roared.

"Your honor, we went to New Orleans on a flatboat, and we started north on the Trace. We lost our horses and one man. We didn't have any money. We were tired, and we wanted to come home."

The judge looked at him dubiously.

"If you wanted to get home," Roger said abruptly, "why did you come back to break into my place that night?"

The judge lifted his craggy eyebrows. "He did that?"

Roger said, "I don't know for sure that this man was among them, your honor. I do know there were several of them came back, and one tried to climb in the window."

"What happened to him?"

"My boy Jeff shot him through the heart."

"At night?"

"Yes."

"Moonlight?"

"No."

"How far?"

"About two hundred yards, your honor."

The judge looked pleased. "Mighty good shootin'," he observed.

The crowd laughed. Somebody had a jug, and it was going from hand to hand.

"Now, then," the judge said, coming down on the front legs of the chair with a crack, "I want to make a little talk—and this is for your benefit, Mr. McClanahan."

The young attorney prudently kept still.

"This ain't like any court you ever saw, maybe. I been east, and I seen the judges with powdered wigs and big law books sit around and listen while the lawyers argued. But this country ain't like Massachusetts. This here country is full of growin' pains. The law ain't caught up with us yet in all its foofarraw. If we let you dandified young fellers come in here and tangle us up, the outlaws and the forces of evil would run every honest man out of the country, after first stealing his horses, taking his scalp, and raping his wife. Now we don't aim to have that happen. We've had plenty of trouble but we're cleaning it up as fast as we can. This court is short on legal larnin' but long on justice. I helped catch this thief and I recognized the brand. He's guilty and I know he's guilty. Under sich circumstances I am going to see that he is sentenced."

"Yes, your honor," McClanahan said meekly.

"Now, mister," said the judge, "where you from?"

"I came from western Pennsylvania."

"Serve in the war?"

"Yes, your honor."

"Whose regiment?" the judge asked sharply.

"I—well—I was with Francis Marion."

The judge called out to the back of the room. "Mr. Mountjoy."

A man with a jug in his hand arose. "Yes, your honor."

148

"Was you with Marion?"

"Yes, your honor."

"Ever see the prisoner before?"

The man squinted. "I don't think so, your honor."

"Maybe," the judge said beguilingly, "you better tell us exactly where you was at during the war."

The prisoner's eyes dropped. "I was in Tarleton's brigade, your honor. I deserted just before the battle of Cowpens and went to the Ohio Country."

The judge was indignant. "A Tory, eh? And a damned Tory deserter, at that!" He snorted. "Prisoner at the bar, I find you guilty of horse-thievery, and I sentence you to be confined in the public pillory for one hour, to have both your ears nailed to the pillory for one hour, to have both cut off at the end of that hour; to receive thirty-nine lashes on your bare back with a cowhide soaked in salt water, to be branded on your right cheek with an H and on your left cheek with a T. Sentence to begin at noon."

"Your honor." McClanahan was on his feet. "I protest the severity of this sentence!"

"It's a severe country." The judge worked his quid around to the other side of his mouth. "A man can be hung."

McClanahan, now thoroughly pale, sat down.

The judge said, "Anybody got any good horses to swap, I'll be at the Jackson Livery until the afternoon session."

Roger stayed to watch the sentence executed. The thief was confined in the pillory, with feet, hands, and head in the holes, while men and small boys jeered at him, and not a few expectorated scornfully and with considerable precision. Two men held the thief's head while the sheriff pushed the upper part of the thief's ear back against the pillory and pounded a big square nail through it and into the wood. A little blood dripped down on the prisoner's shoulder. Then the sheriff went to the other side and nailed the other ear, and the man's head was forced up and back in an awkward position. The sheriff took his hammer and went back to his log cabin office, while blood dripped from both the prisoner's ears, and big blueflies buzzed around his head.

At the end of an hour the sheriff appeared with a long blacksnake whip with a two-foot cowhide lash. He carried it coiled, and brine dripping from the bottom of the coils made an intermittent trail on the dusty ground. The sheriff saw that both the man's ears were still nailed. He went around behind, took a stand, and rolled out the whip. He gauged his distance and found he was too close. He took a step backward. Somebody with a sharp knife slit the man's shirt from top to bottom and laid it open so his back was bare. The sheriff, a big man, measured his distance again. He snapped his wrist. The long length of the blacksnake rose in the air, sailed over his shoulder, and trailed out behind him. Then he swung his big arm with all the force of his torso. The wet whip whistled in the air. It hit the man's bare back with a loud smack, and the lash curled around the man's body, with the end of it stopping around his stomach with a sound like the crack of a pistol. The man went rigid and strained against the heavy boards of the pillory.

The whip descended again. The man's eyes were closed. On the third stroke he jerked his head and tore one ear, but the nail held and the ear only bled more freely.

The audience was silent, watching each motion of the whip, holding its breath as the lash cut away the skin on the man's stomach. The real damage, though, was on his back, where the heaviness of the whip macerated skin and flesh. His back was bleeding freely at the sixth strike, and the sheriff gave the whip to another man.

At the eighteenth stroke the prisoner no longer had the strength to go rigid. "O God!" he cried. "Why don't you shoot me and have it over with?"

"Shootin's too good for a horse thief!" somebody said, and Judge Wilson, watching the whip, counted: "Nineteen."

Some twenty feet in front of the pillory, the blacksmith built up a fire to heat the branding irons.

The prisoner began to moan and then to blubber. A spasm ran through him at every lash of the whip, and finally he seemed to go limp and unconscious. The sheriff looked at Wilson for instructions. "I said thirty-nine," the judge reminded him, and the lash continued to be laid on.

By now there was a large crowd of men and boys and some women. The dogs chased one another, barking, and the members of the audience talked to one another between lashes, but at the moment the stroke was laid on there was complete silence, so the smack of the lash sounded loud and clear. Finally the prisoner's back was a lacerated, bloody mass. The judge counted thirty-nine and nodded, satisfied.

The blacksmith approached with one of the cherry red irons. Somebody in the crowd shouted, "Wake him up first!"

"He'll come to," the judge predicted.

He did. As the glowing iron was squeezed into his cheek, the prisoner shrieked. The blacksmith backed away, scrutinizing his work critically. Smoke from burning skin and tissue arose from the iron. He seemed satisfied, and went for the second iron.

The prisoner seemed to go temporarily insane. He screamed and gurgled and threw himself against the stocks. His wrists and ankles and neck began to bleed.

But the sheriff got him by the hair and held his head back solidly against the pillory. The smith pressed the second iron against his other cheek. The prisoner fainted again.

Then the sheriff took a scalping knife from a sheath on his belt, and sliced off the tops of both ears so the man's head would be free.

The judge waved his hand. "Turn 'im loose." He glared at the crowd. "Let that be a lesson to any of you who covets your neighbor's horse." He added under his breath, "The damned Tory!"

11 IT WAS LATE IN THE EVENING when Roger reached home. The Trace was beginning to settle up now. There was a family every two or three miles—a far cry from 1783, when he had been the first one south of Nashville.

He turned the chestnut into the pen and went in. They were eating supper. He surveyed Anne and the three younger children. "Where's Jeff?" he asked.

Anne hesitated. "He's out hunting."

Roger looked at her. He felt mean—mean at himself, mean at the world. He knew why too. As much as he understood the necessity of violent punishment in a violent land, he guessed he was getting soft. The whipping, branding and ear-cropping of the horse thief had seemed unnecessarily severe. There had to be severity, of course, or the outlaws would take over, and he faced the fact that, with the increasing traffic of returning riverman up the Trace, many of them carrying large amounts of gold, even more severity might be necessary in the future. The frontier had not been conquered. Lawlessness was merely shifting from Kentucky to the Trace. There was, practically speaking, no law south of Nashville. Even in Natchez, down on the river, there was no one with authority to perform a marriage.

It was to be anticipated, then, that a strong arm would be called for. The experience with the five travelers was only the beginning.

Jeff did not come in until late that night, and brought no game. Roger was inclined to question, but thought better of it. Indeed he was getting edgy, when he couldn't trust a boy like Jeff in the forest. Jeff was the quiet type, and in the forest he was like an Indian.

The camp meetings up in Tennessee and Kentucky went full blast in the summer of 1801; people by the thousands camped in tents around a meeting ground; they labored all day in prayer and meditation, and listened all night to sometimes twenty or thirty preachers exhorting from different stumps, urging the sinners to confess and enter the grace of the Lord. An epidemic of the jerks went through the country, and even appeared at dances and house-warmings. People had visions and talked in tongues. On the other side of the fence, there was sometimes considerable drinking and rowdyism, and it was said that more than one supposedly innocent girl came home pregnant.

Roger didn't go to camp meetings. He said they'd better be more concerned with observing the Golden Rule, and Anne agreed with him. Besides, it was a busy summer. There was not only the corn to look after, but ever more travelers were coming up the Trace, and Roger waited for the first major outbreak of lawlessness.

Travelers complained of minor thefts, most of which they blamed on the Indians, and it was standard practice to hide their gold, if they had any, in the bushes at night to avoid losing it if they should be visited by robbers. Up and down the Trace, the neighbors too seemed to fear what was coming. They met one night at Roger's place and organized a regular company of Regulators, electing Virgil Coates captain.

Shortly after, a man named Joshua Baker came up the Trace on a lathered horse, telling Coates he had been held up by four armed men headed by a man named Mason.

Roger was there helping Coates with a foundered horse at the time. Coates held the horse down while Roger, his arm smeared with deer tallow, dug handful after handful out of the horse's intestines.

The man Baker said that he and two others were robbed of twenty-three hundred dollars; that the four men had their faces blacked, but he recognized Samuel Mason, for he was a big fellow, "weighing about two forty," and didn't look like a highwayman.

"Mason," Roger said slowly, "used to be at Cave-in-Rock between Kentucky and Indiana Territory."

"I've seen Mason," said Baker, "and I'm sure this was him. I didn't know the ones with him, but the leader was Mason, all right."

"They took your money," said Roger, reaching for the tallow. "Why didn't you get up a posse and go after them down there?"

"We did—and they waylaid us. We was lucky to get off with our lives."

"What do you want us to do?" asked Coates.

"I'm just warning you. Last time we saw them, Mason's gang was headed this way."

"Did you hear where his headquarters are?"

"In Natchez they say he lives in a cave at Rocky Springs, northeast of Natchez, but nobody knows for sure."

"That's quite a ways off," Coates observed. "It doesn't exactly seem to be our responsibility."

"It *will* be," said Baker. "Them fellows will be up on the Trace as far as the state line before you know it."

"We'll keep a watch," said Coates.

The riverboat men continued to trail northward, some on horses, some afoot, some whipsawing. Some reported robberies, occasionally of good sums, but mostly they were hungry and tired and short on clothing. These Roger fed when they came by his place, but he kept a sharp eye on them.

In March, 1802, Coates rode up to Roger's place on a lathered horse. Roger was mauling some fence rails out of logs he had dragged in from an oak grove over beyond the ridge where Charles was buried, and he stopped in his work long enough to cock an eye at Coates.

"I'd say you're in somewhat of a stew."

Coates nodded. "You'll be too," he said breathlessly. "There's a dead man on the Trace."

Roger, hit the wedge once more with the axe, and the oak rived with a cracking sound. "Where is it?"

"Couple of miles the other side of old man Hammond's."

Roger went back to the horse pen and got a bridle. He went out in the stubblefield and called the chestnut. He got him saddled and went in the house for his rifle. Anne watched him with eyes large. "Trouble, Roger?"

"Not too much right now, far as I know—but we might have to look around in the brush."

She said nothing, but looked worried, and it struck him that she too was getting older. These things hurt her more than they had. He patted her shoulder. "No danger," he said. "We're just going to investigate."

They joined up with old man Hammond and Kuykendall and two brothers named Duncan and an old bachelor, Hiram Hall, who lived below Coates.

"My dogs found the body this mornin'," said Hammond. "I heard them barkin' and seen the buzzards circlin' and came down to have a look."

"Move the body?" asked Roger.

"No. Left it right where it was. Just turned it over to have a look, then let it roll back on its face. It was cold last night, and the body was stiff."

"Know him?"

"Never saw him before—far as I know."

"What do you mean, far as you know?" Roger asked sharply.

"You'll see. This gent might be a little hard to recognize anywhere, shape he's in."

Roger didn't answer. He didn't know what Hammond was driving at, but it didn't sound good. Most of all, it didn't sound good for the Trace. Only two miles below Coates'; that was a smart piece from Natchez, and it meant not only that the outlaws were getting bolder but that they were ranging farther. It was the way it always had been: the robbers and the killers went as far as they were allowed to go; you had to drive them out with steel and lead; that was the only language they understood.

The body lay at the foot of a big catalpa tree. Roger scrutinized it. There was blood on the left side of the face. He got down and turned the body over. He looked at the face and swallowed. The whole left side had been taken off, as if a bear had taken a tremendous swipe at him.

"Devil's claws," said Hall. "I seen 'em before."

Roger looked for a bullet hole. There was none. "It seems to me the man bled to death," he said.

Coates said, "If we got that kind of killers around, we better guard our families."

Roger studied the corpse. The man must have been raked several times with the claws, for the flesh was nearly all cleaned off of the left side of his face, done to the bone. The left eye was gone, and the cheekbone shone pinkish white in the sun.

"Look for papers?" asked Roger.

"No papers," said Hammond. "No money neither."

"How'd he get here?" asked Roger. "From the looks of his shoes, he wasn't doing much walking."

"If he had a horse, they took it—whoever killed him."

Roger drew a deep breath and looked up and down the trail. Yes, he thought, this was the kind of thing he could fight. Things inside of you or the things you feared might happen to you—those were hard to combat, but this, a man roaming the forest with a rifle and a knife and a set of devil's claws—this was something he understood and could do something about. He looked back at the body. "We better be sure there are no papers, then bury him."

Coates examined the body while Hiram Hall studied the ground. Coates shook his head, "There's not a thing. If he had anything, the outlaws took it."

Hall spoke up. "They was two of 'em. They went back south, leadin' his horse."

They got shovels at Hall's and dug a grave.

"I got a blanket to cover him," Hall said. "A man hadn't ought to have clods throwed in his face."

They filled in the grave. "You better keep a record of this," Roger told Coates. "Put down his description the best you can—his one eye was gray—and the date and where he was found. He may have people back home somewhere—maybe a wife and kids."

"What was he doing on the Trace this time of year?" asked Coates.

"Hard to say. Maybe he got stranded in New Orleans last fall. Maybe he went down in the winter—some do, if the water isn't too low."

They laid some big rocks on top of the grave. "You know," said old man Hammond, leaning on his shovel, "I can't say I like this."

"Who does?" asked Kuykendall, cutting off a chew with his big scalping knife.

"I never seen but two fellers use them devil's claws," Hammond went on. "One was Little Harpe and the other was Sam Mason's son-in-law." He paused. "Sam Mason's son-in-law was killed in '94."

In the next month, April, there was a big to-do, for Joshua Baker was robbed again by Mason at the mouth of the Yazoo River. Baker was taking a cargo downriver on a flatboat, and two canoes, filled with six men each, approached him and wanted to buy firearms. Baker refused to let them approach and fired on them. After a running gun fight, the outlaws had been beaten off, but Baker had recognized two of them. He drifted on down the river to Natchez and reported to Governor Claiborne, who promptly alerted the three military units in his area and offered a reward of nine hundred dollars for the capture of Samuel Mason and Wiley Harpe!

This news ran up and down the Trace like fire in a dry canebrake. They held a meeting at Virgil Coates' place one night in early May.

"It sure don't sound good to me," said one of the Duncans. "I knew that Harpe feller was goin' to turn up somewhere sooner or later, but I hoped it wouldn't be on the Trace."

"Now he's with Mason," Hiram Hall said, "he'll be twice as hard. That Mason has a big gang. He has look-outs in Nashville and Natchez, and there's a merchant in Natchez who takes his stolen goods off of him."

"The thing is," Coates demanded, "what are we going to do about it?"

"There is only one answer to that," said Roger. "Keep our powder dry."

"It would be different," said old man Hammond, "if we wuz a part of some other state, but right in here we don't belong to nothin'. We're too far south to be in Tennessee and too far north to be in Mississippi Territory."

Hiram Hall said, "I thought we belonged to North Carolina."

Kuykendall spit on the ground. "Technically speakin', yes—but it don't do us any good."

"It doesn't make much difference," Roger pointed out. "They get robbed and killed right around Natchez."

The hunt for Mason spread through the Natchez area. Men and dogs went out looking for Samuel Mason, for he, while perhaps not as bloody a killer as Wiley Harpe, had been a criminal for a long time, and had committed enough robberies and murders to swing ten times in hell. Also, Mason was shrewd. He had an organization. He had been forced out of Cave-in-Rock on the same wave of outlaw-hunting that had destroyed Micajah Harpe, and following which Wiley Harpe, the red-haired one, had disappeared. Where had Little Harpe been for the last three years? None knew, but it was a common guess that he had been killing and stealing. Now suddenly he showed up as a member of Mason's gang, and it was something to be alarmed at. Wiley Harpe, the unpredictable killer, backed by Mason's organization! But Mason had vanished, and nobody claimed the reward. That Christmas Roger gave Jeff a new rifle with a black curly maple stock. He was to remember that.

In January, 1803, Mason was arrested by the Spanish at Little Prairie, six hundred miles above Natchez. According to reports, no man by the name of Harpe was with him. The Spanish sent them all to New Orleans, but there the officials decided that Mason's crimes had been committed on the American side of the river, and Governor Salcedo wrote Clairborne that he would send Mason to Natchez for trial.

But in March, one hundred miles below Natchez, Mason and his entire gang escaped. A week later they were seen northeast of Natchez.

Holdups occurred more frequently along the Trace—some within a few miles of Roger's cabin. He turned his dogs loose at night, and made sure that Coates had dogs around his place. Bodies were found, but nobody knew how many were disposed of and never found. It was common knowledge that Mason had established his headquarters near Natchez. It was said also that Little Harpe was with him, but nobody could lay a finger on them. Those whom they robbed did not live to identify them.

Jeff, these days, was gone a good deal during the day, and Roger asked him why. "I'm looking for Mason and Harpe," he said.

Roger studied him. Jeff was almost as tall as he was, though slender. And he could split a bullet on a knife blade at sixty yards. But Roger shook his head. "These men are murderers—professional killers. They don't know the meaning of fair play. You wouldn't have a chance."

"I would," said Jeff, "if I got the first shot."

"Well, maybe they won't come up here."

But he knew better. They were already up there. Almost daily now a body was found on the Trace—sometimes more than one. Men went to Nashville, when they had to go, in companies. None traveled the Trace alone but John Swaney, the mailman. He reported meeting Mason more than once, but the big man didn't bother him. He asked for the news and Swaney told him. He asked what they were saying about him in the settlements, and laughed when he heard about the reward offered. He laughed too when Little Harpe's name was mentioned.

"Funny thing," Swaney told Roger one morning, "he acts like he's tellin' the truth when he says Little Harpe isn't one of his men."

"Harpe has been identified two or three times," said Roger.

"Well, the only thing I can figger is that Harpe is usin' another name. Maybe Mason doesn't even know who Harpe is."

"Maybe." Roger dropped his axe. "Come in and we'll have a cup of spicewood tea."

"I might, at that. Not too long, though. I've got tracks to make before dark."

"There's water on. It won't take but a minute."

They went into the big cabin. Anne, barefooted and

silent, smiled at Mr. Swaney and went about brewing the tea. "Maybe," said Roger, "Mr. Swaney would like a chunk of that deer loin you roasted last night."

She looked up. "I gave that to Jeff this morning. He said he was going hunting."

Roger frowned slowly. "For a boy that hunts all the time, he sure doesn't bring home much meat," he said.

12 A NEW FAMILY had moved onto old man Hammond's land, and Roger rode with Swaney down to visit. He found the usual barefooted man wearing a shapeless felt hat made of buffalo wool, a skin-toughened woman, and half a dozen small kids.

"My name's Adams," said Roger. "Live up the Trace a way."

The man eyed him suspiciously. The woman watched from the doorway. The kids watched from all over.

"This is Swaney, the mailman," said Roger. "You'll be seeing him."

The man looked carefully at Swaney's leather pouch. "You got letters in there?"

"Sure." Swaney took out a handful, spread them, and put them back in the wallet.

"Maybe it's all right, then," the man said, "but they warned me in Nashville to watch out for tricks."

"Don't blame you," Roger said.

"This here Mason, they say, is a mighty smooth feller."

"But he's mainly after big money—travelers going up the Trace."

"How about this Little Harpe?"

Roger looked around him into the woods. "Different story," he said finally. "You never know where or how Harpe may strike. He's a born killer and a shrewd one.

Sometimes he kills for money, sometimes for fun, more often both. What's your name?"

"Silas Nicholson."

"Where you from, Si?"

"No'th Carolina."

Roger turned the chestnut, not having been asked to alight. "Need any help," he said, "let somebody know. We're all neighbors down here. We never—"

He stopped, head up. A shot had sounded back up the Trace in the direction from which they had just come.

"Somebody huntin'," said Swaney. "Well, see you in two weeks, Roger."

"Sure." Roger's eyes were scanning the forest. "Sure. Stop by." He started off at a trot.

Half a mile up the trail he found the body, still warm. The body was of a boy, not over seventeen, and he had been on foot. Roger backtrailed him. The boy had camped beyond the trail. He had built a fire that morning and had cooked some potatoes and a haunch of venison. He must have had a rifle then. But what was he starting so late in the day for? It was almost noon. He had had a horse, but it was gone now. Had the horse maybe gotten loose in the cane and delayed his start that morning?

Roger went back to the body and got down. He tied the chestnut's reins to a bough overhead, and bent to examine the body. The boy had been shot just above the heart. Probably, then, he had been shot back at his camp and had run out to the trail before he died.

He had been shot from in front. That argued that someone had approached him in the guise of friendship. That wasn't too easy to figure out, for wouldn't any man traveling the Trace alone in 1803 be warned a hundred times of outlaws? Of course there were other ways it could have happened, but Roger shook his head. There was something about this he didn't like at all.

He examined the boy's pockets but found nothing. As usual, there was no way to identify him, so there would be nobody at home to notify and nobody to kick up a fuss about his death. Roger picked up the body. The boy had been tall and slender, something like Jeff. He'd gone down the river to see New Orleans. He must have had money too, for he'd had a horse of his own.

He turned into Coates' place a little later. Liz appeared in the door and started to smile. Then she saw the body and turned white. "Virgil's down by the creek digging turnips," she said.

"Maybe you'd better blow your horn."

She blew it, and presently Virgil came up, with the twins, barefooted, in their wamuses, behind him.

"I got something down the road," Roger said.

Virgil shook his head. "Young feller, too. How far down the road?"

"Mile or so." Roger slid the body down to the ground. Virgil studied him. "No papers, I suppose."

Roger shook his head. He told what he had found. Virgil said, "We'll bury him. All I can do is put it down. Some day maybe we'll get to the bottom of these things."

"When we do," Roger said harshly, "somebody will hang."

Virgil was grim as he straightened: "This is one too many," he said. "No matter who did it—Harpe or anybody else—we're going to get him."

Roger went home and got to work digging a cistern. The old one had caved in. He went inside after a while and watched Anne's strong, quick fingers braiding rawhide strips into a rope. It seemed to him he had known Anne all of his life, and every hour of it had been good. She was a strong and willing woman, quick to learn. She had come with her parents from Maryland, one of the first white children in Kentucky. Then her father had gone back to fight in the war and had been killed by Cornwallis' men before the surrender of Yorktown.

She had never known anything but the frontier; she had grown up on it and had been a part of it. Women like her had a great deal to do with making America what it was.

She must have sensed his thought, for she looked up and smiled.

For some strange reason he didn't want to leave her, but this was the West and there was always work to do. He went back to the cistern.

That night at supper he looked at her, across the table from him, in the firelight. Jeff and Will were on one side; Betty and Sarah on the other. Roger said,

"You'd all best stay close to the house for a while. Outlawry is on the increase. The spring flatboatmen are coming back up the Trace, and it is worth a man's life to travel alone."

Will asked, "Is it like Indians, Papa?"

"It is worse than Indians," he told them heavily, "for you never know who it is. When Indians were on the warpath, we were always on guard. With white men on the warpath but acting like friends—" he shook his head. "It cannot go on."

"Will they catch 'im, Papa?"

"They will catch them all eventually—but before they do, some good men will be killed."

Anne began to look concerned. "Was there somebody today?"

He nodded. "Below Liz's place. A boy about seventeen. No papers. Don't know who his folks were, where he lived—anything."

Anne's lips were tight. She shook her head slowly. "His folks will wonder for years."

Virgil Coates came up to the house four days later. Roger was putting up hollowed-out half-logs as rain gutters to fill the cistern. Coates got down from his horse, and the twins rode into the yard behind him. They were two years old now, and rode a small pony, old and rock-steady, with nothing but a tow-sack over its back to keep the salt from galling their legs. It didn't need a bridle because it would follow Coates' horse—a little slowly, but always there. Hughie, the

169

boy, sat in front and hung onto the horse's mane, while Jane, the girl, kept her arms tightly around her brother.

Roger got down from the hogshead he was standing on, and lifted the two kids to the ground.

"Reckon we'll have to put up a mounting block for you two," he said. Hughie nodded offhandedly, while Jane looked at him with her big eyes. Then Anne, in the doorway, called to the children, and they went in.

"How's the corn?" asked Roger, getting back up on the barrel.

"Corn is good," Coates said, and the shortness of his answer made Roger look around at him.

"Something eating on you?" he asked.

Coates said, "Maybe."

Roger got back down from the hogshead. "I'm listening."

Coates watched his horse wander off toward the cane followed by the kids' pony. "I don't know just how to say this to you, Roger."

Roger squinted a little as he scrutinized Coates, for the sun was in his eyes. He began to tighten up. "Maybe some plain talk would do the job," he suggested.

"Maybe. I—"

Roger waited. Coates didn't go on. "Something against me?" Roger suggested.

Coates squatted at the corner of the house. He found a piece of cedar from the rain gutters Roger was putting up, and took out his scalping knife and began to whittle on it. "Where's Jeff?" he asked finally.

"Jeff is grubbing out cane down the creek."

They had knocked out the chinking to provide summer ventilation, and Roger could hear Anne talking to the twins. Marie was singing some strange Haitian song as she worked in the kitchen cabin. The other blacks were pulling weeds in the corn, and Roger's three youngest children were helping. Roger had four hundred acres in corn that year.

"Well, you know how it is," Coates said. "They elected me captain of the Regulators, and I'm sworn to do my duty no matter who is involved."

Roger turned his head sidewise to look better at him. "If I've done something," he said slowly, "you better go ahead and do your duty. I won't stop you. You've been a good husband to Liz and I've got no cause to think you'll ever be anything else. So if you've got something against me, spit it out."

A chip of cedar flew across the yard. "It ain't you," said Coates. "It's Jeff!"

Roger's mouth opened, but he didn't say anything right away. He watched Coates and saw the man was terribly in earnest and sweating profusely, even in the shade, and he felt sorry for him, but at the same time a feeling of dread began to creep over him like the iciness from a north wind. "If Jeff's been up to something he'll have to stand good for it."

"I figgered that's the way you'd feel, but that don't make it easy."

"You aren't trying to tell me Jeff's been—stealing something!" He had to force the words out of his throat.

Coates breathed so deep his stomach moved. "I might as well tell you the whole thing."

"You might as well."

"There's been talk about Jeff for some time now—him being away during the day so much and all."

"Jeff likes to hunt."

"He been bringin' home much meat lately?"

That stunned Roger for a moment. "All right, what are they saying?"

It came with the suddenness of a Mississippi typhoon, and exploded with as much force. "They say he's been in on these holdups along the Trace!"

Roger felt as if he had been hit in the back of the head with a grubbing hoe. At first he was numb, and then he was cold all over. He tried to find his cob pipe in the wallet of his overlapped shirt, but his fingers were numb and he couldn't feel. He withdrew his hand and faced Coates, his thin face taut. "Any evidence?"

"Maybe." Coates seemed relieved, now that he had said it.

"It doesn't seem—it isn't—"

"I know how you feel, Roger. I don't like it any more than you do, but the neighbors—"

"You don't have to apologize," Roger said harshly. "Law has to be upheld."

"They don't think he's in it alone."

Roger got up, his eyes looking off over the forest, not seeing. "Maybe, maybe not. What's the evidence?"

"Jeff has been seen around places where these holdups have happened—places where he really hasn't got any business being."

"Who's seen him?"

"You remember that boy you found below my place?"

Roger froze for an instant. "Yes."

"Mrs. Nicholson took one of the kids outside right after that shot, and saw Jeff loping up a draw leading a mouse-colored dun horse. Leastwise, she thought it was Jeff. Said she'd seen him several times, once close up, and her description sounds like Jeff, all right."

"It could be a mistake," Roger said.

"It could be. The horse ain't a mistake. This boy bought corn from Nicholson the day before, and Nicholson remembers the horse."

Roger felt suddenly empty. "Where would Jeff take a horse? He hasn't brought it home."

One of the twins began to cry, and he heard Anne's soothing voice as she calmed the child. He raised his head to listen, and from the cane came the crash of the grubbing hoe.

"That's why they say there's a gang."

Roger shook his head, trying to think. "Jeff never has come home with anything that I know of—no money, no rifles." He looked up. "That's one thing that Jeff would like—a rifle. If there'd be anything he'd want out of a situation like that, it would be a rifle. But he's got a good rifle."

"You better look into it."

Roger got up, dusting the seat of his pants. "I'll let you know in a week or two."

Coates got up too, but he was frowning. "It better be sooner than that."

"Is there a hurry?" Roger asked.

"There's a hurry. The men are sayin' Jeff killed the boy down on the Trace. You better find out today."

"I don't think—Jeff wouldn't—"

"You never know," said Coates. "All these outlaws was kids onct, and some of 'em came from good families, like yourn."

"But Jeff is quiet."

"Quietness can cover up a lot of things," Coates reminded him. "I say you never can tell, and if a man is accused he'd better be ready to defend himself."

Roger closed his eyes tightly for a minute. "I'll find out today. If there's any question about it, I'll see he's turned over. I don't want anything like that hanging over his head."

Coates went to the door and called the twins. Anne looked at the two men and asked, "What's wrong?"

"Nothing yet," said Roger, and started for the cane-brake.

13 THROUGH THE KITCHEN DOOR Adams saw Marie with a sleeping child on her lap, while she sang on and on. He turned and saw Coates ride out of the yard, with the old pony behind him. He heard the steady sound of chopping ahead, and went on down to the cane.

Jeff looked up as his father approached, but he went ahead with his chopping. Roger noted that he swung the grubbing hoe easily, and realized that Jeff had built up considerable strength. He watched him get the blade under a cane root and pry it out.

"This stuff will make a good fire in the fall," he said.

Jeff grunted and kept on working. Roger watched him, but could tell nothing from his manner. Roger looked up the hill toward the blacks working in the corn. Beyond the corn a quarter of a mile was the Trace proper; this way it was lower ground, down toward the Tennessee River. He heard a bluejay scolding, and looked back at Jeff. "Hunting any good lately?"

"Not much." Jeff didn't stop.

"It ought to be a good year," Roger said. "Lots of feed, plenty of rabbits."

"Too many settlers," Jeff said. "They're driving the game out of the country."

Roger was looking around. Jeff's horse was fattening on the cane; it was saddled and bridled.

Jeff pried up another root; it gave way with a crunching sound.

"Where's your rifle?" asked Roger.

"I keep it around," Jeff said.

Roger hated having to do this. "Thought I'd like to take a shot with it," he said.

Jeff stopped. "You've got a rifle."

"Maybe I want to shoot yours."

Jeff straightened up suddenly, fire in his eyes. "Can't I have something of my own—just once?"

Roger studied him. "Just once," he repeated slowly. "Is it your feeling that you've never had anything to yourself?"

"Nobody does in this wilderness."

Roger considered for a moment. This was a side Jeff never had shown him before. "I didn't know you felt that way."

"How could anybody feel any other way?"

"Life on the frontier," Roger said, "is not easy. What we have, we all have. It seems to me you've had your share."

"Is that all a man is supposed to have—a share?"

Roger looked at him. "I want to see that rifle," he said.

"It's over there." Jeff jerked his head.

Roger looked at him and then at the big sycamore tree which he had indicated. He saw nothing of the rifle. He started toward the tree.

Jeff passed him, running. From somewhere in long grass near the foot of the tree he snatched up a rifle. He pointed it at Roger and said, "Go away and leave me alone. I'm doing my work. You leave me alone."

Roger stopped. "Do you realize you're pointing that rifle at me?"

"I know what I'm doing," said Jeff.

"Then put down that rifle and quit acting the fool."

Jeff sighted the rifle on Roger's chest. "Go back to the house and leave me alone."

Roger said quietly, "You know I'm not going to do that now?"

"You'd better if you know what's good for you."

"And be backed down by my own boy?" Roger stepped toward him. "Put down that rifle and talk."

"Don't come closer!"

Roger didn't break his slow stride. "Behave yourself. Put down that rifle."

It wavered a little. Roger grasped the muzzle end. He jerked it away from Jeff. "Sit down," he said. "Sit down and talk. You've got things to explain."

Jeff looked sullen. "What?"

"Why you pointed a rifle at me, for one thing?" Roger was examining the rifle. "Why you've got a different rifle, for another."

"It's my rifle. It's none of your business how I got it."

"I'll make it my business," said Roger. He put the rifle to his shoulder and fired it into the cane. Then he took the belt from around his hunting shirt. "I'm going to give you the licking of your life," he said, and swung the heavy cowhide.

Jeff charged him. Roger brushed him off the first

177

time, but Jeff gained confidence and came back with more strength. They closed. Roger got a leg behind him and forced him back. Jeff flailed at his face, fingernails spread, but Roger kept his head back out of the way. He got Jeff on his stomach and held him there with his left hand between his shoulder blades while he whaled him with all the strength of his right arm. It took about thirty licks to whip the fight out of him, and it took another ten to get him where Roger wanted him.

"You never whipped me like that before," Jeff sobbed. "When a boy points his rifle at a man, he's lucky to get off with a strapping."

Roger backed away. The rifle was still on the ground. Roger caught movement and looked up. Anne was standing on a high point a little above them, and he saw the terrible anxiety in her dark eyes under the calico sundown. "It's all right," he said. "Go back to the house."

She turned reluctantly, and the wind billowed her long dress as she went back up the hill. Roger watched Jeff get to his feet. "Now about the rifle," he said.

"I traded for it."

"Where?"

"One of the fellows down the Trace."

"Who?"

"I traded from Jake Sawyer just before he went on to Natchez."

Roger glanced at the rifle. "Jake Sawyer never had as fancy a rifle as that, and he never had a bluish colored stock with a silver star with four straight points."

"I got it from him," Jeff said stubbornly.

"I could whip you and make you tell," Roger said, "but I'm not going to do it that way. If you got this rifle where the neighbors think you got it, you're in trouble—plenty of trouble."

Jeff didn't answer. Roger picked up the rifle. He balanced it in his hand and went after the horse. "Come on," he said to Jeff.

Marie stopped singing as they made their way past the kitchen cabin up to the main cabin. Roger handed the rifle to Anne. "I want you to put that away and keep it put away. Don't let anybody see it and don't tell anybody about it."

She took the rifle, looking fearful. Roger went to get the chestnut. "Get on your horse," he told Jeff, "and lead out toward Coates' place."

Coates was slopping hogs. "You find out anything?"

"Maybe." Roger saw Liz staring at them from the door, and the twins watching from behind her skirts. "Going to have another?" he asked Coates.

"Seems as though."

"We're going down to Nicholson's. Want to go along?"

"Sure." He saddled up a big plowhorse and they went out to the Trace and started down it. "Know Jake Sawyer?" asked Roger.

"Some."

"What kind of rifle did he have?"

"Jake? Seems to me his rifle had a butt piece whittled out of cedar—but I might be mistaken. Prob'ly not, though. Jake was sorta lazy, and oak was too hard for him to whittle."

It was midafternoon when they got to Nicholson's. His wife, barefooted, said she allowed they'd find him over the hill looking for ginseng.

"It's too early to dig," Roger said.

"It ain't too early to look."

They went on over the hill and found Nicholson roaming through the woods with a rifle on his shoulder. "Thought I might get a shot at a squirrel—" He stopped short when he saw Jeff.

"Did you know Jake Sawyer?" asked Roger.

"Sure. Him and me come from the same town in Virginia, up along the Pennsylvania line."

"Know what kind of rifle he had?"

"He only had one, and he broke the stock last winter. He whittled a new one out of a piece of soft pine."

"Do you know what he did with it when he went to Natchez?"

"Last I saw of him, he still had it. Fact, he crippled a deer just above my place, and stopped to tell me about it, so he must of had it."

"He crippled this deer on the way to Natchez?"

"That's the way I said it."

"Do you recall what kind of rifle Jeff here has?"

Nicholson scratched his head. "Nice rifle—nothing fancy. I've seen it plenty of time. Black stock, warn't it?"

"Plain or decorated?"

"Plain as far as I know."

"One more question. Did that boy we found up the trail stop here five nights ago?"

"He sure did. He bought a piece of hog and some corn for his horse."

"Did he have a rifle?"

"He did that. A right party thing with a bluish stock and a silver star with four points."

Roger took a deep breath and leaned for a moment on his saddlehorn. Finally he turned to Coates. "Jeff is your prisoner—but I'd like to talk to him first."

"I don't see why not."

"He's a killer," said Nicholson quickly. "You better not take any chances on him."

"There won't be any chances," Roger said heavily. "I will stand good for him in person."

Coates shook his head. "Be careful what you do. You're layin' yourself open."

"You'll have him," Roger said, "before sundown."

Coates rode out ahead, and presently, when he was out of hearing, Roger spoke to Jeff in front of him, "Could you tell me why you did it, Jeff?"

"He had a nice rifle," said Jeff.

"So did you."

"I took a notion to his."

"Then tell me this: how did you know he had this rifle?"

Jeff looked startled for a moment. "I saw it," he said finally.

"What happened to the horse?"

"I turned it loose. I didn't need a horse."

181

"You're lying," said Roger. "You needed a horse more than you needed a rifle."

Jeff didn't answer.

Roger went on. "Who else was in it with you?"

"Nobody."

"I don't believe that."

"You don't think I've got enough guts to do a thing like that."

Roger said soberly, "It seems obvious that you have. But how did you get started? You didn't decide all by yourself to kill this boy."

"Why not?"

"You haven't been raised that way."

"Does raising make a difference?"

For a while Roger was silent, thinking. "Maybe you're right," he said. "Maybe it doesn't make any difference—but it still looks to me as if you weren't in it alone. You say you turned the boy's horse loose— but nobody has reported finding it."

"It's got the whole West to get lost in."

"That's true, but it's surprising how an animal like a horse can't stay out of sight very long, even in this country."

"What would I do with it, then?"

"The way it looks to me, you took the rifle, and the other fellow took the horse. Maybe he took the horse down to Natchez to sell it."

"What difference does it make?"

"It might make a lot. Do you realize what you're in for?"

"Thirty-nine lashes on the bare back, I suppose."

Roger said, "It won't be that easy."

Jeff jerked around to stare at him. "Who said thirty-nine lashes are easy?"

"They're easy compared to what's waiting for you if they find you guilty of shooting that boy."

"What do you think they'll do?" asked Jeff.

"They'll hang you by the neck," Roger said quietly.

That hit Jeff like a bullet between the shoulders. He thought about it for a moment, and then he slowed his horse and dropped back. His sullenness was gone. Now he was scared. "Will it help any if I tell who was in it with me?"

"I don't know," said Roger. "It might. It might not. The best thing I can say is come clean. If you tell everything, they might let you off with thirty-nine lashes."

He saw Jeff jerk as if the blacksnake had wrapped around him. "I'll tell everything I know," he said suddenly.

"Start talking."

"A man named Setton, John Setton. Sometimes he called himself John Taylor."

"Where did you meet him?"

"I come across their camp in the forest one day. Three of them. They were going to kill me and take my rifle, but I talked them out of it, and finally this fellow Setton said I could live if I'd work with them. At first I only had to tell them when somebody with money or a good horse or rifle was coming down the

Trace. Then they took me with them. This time—he told me to do it alone. I thought it would be hard, but it wasn't. He died just like a squirrel or a deer."

Roger closed his eyes for a moment. Then he forced himself to go on. "This Setton—where does he camp?"

"Anywhere. He changes every day."

"How did you get in touch with him?"

"I rode out through the country to the southwest, up on the high ground. They always saw me first."

"Did he take the money of the boy you killed?"

"Yes. I didn't get it."

"You got the rifle?"

"Yes."

"Where is your rifle—the one I gave you a year ago?"

"I tied it up in the top of that big sycamore."

"The first rain would ruin it," Roger observed.

"I figured to move it before that."

"And Setton or Taylor took the horse?"

"Yes."

"What does Setton look like?"

"About my height—not as tall as you. But heavy, tol'able heavy. Sort of scowly looking; never smiled."

"Scowly?"

"Yes."

Roger looked at the forest with unseeing eyes. "What kind of hair did he have?"

"Red, dark red. It was crinkly, and came down low over his eyes."

A while later they turned into Coates' yard. It was still short of sundown. Roger dismounted. "He's your prisoner," he said to Coates.

Liz was at the door, her eyes fixed on Jeff in disbelief. "What's he done, Papa?"

"Got into some trouble," Roger said.

"Get off the horse," Coates said to Jeff.

The boy dismounted slowly. It was coming to him that he was up against something more than a whipping. And high time, Roger thought, although right then he didn't see how he could stand by and see them try him. He remembered how Jeff had always loved to shoot, and surely—no, he looked at Jeff and he knew it wasn't just that he liked guns and shooting. For he had had plenty of that. There was something else that had nothing to do with hunting and shooting, for hunting of itself wasn't bad. A man could put his rifle on his shoulder and walk through the forest on a sunny day in the spring, and he could come home without firing a shot and still feel wonderful. But with Jeff there was something else, and Roger knew it wasn't a thing he could figure out. Of all the children they had had, Jeff had seemed the least likely—he shook his head. "Where you going to keep him?"

"I'll turn that wagon box over on him tonight," Coates said. "Tomorrow we'll have a trial."

"Tomorrow!" Roger himself was shocked. Tomorrow? He began to think back. He remembered how they had put Hughes on trial, and how they had beaten him and torn down his place even after acquittal. He remembered the whipping given to the man who had taken the chestnut, and he knew that tomorrow was right. They had no jails and no place to keep a man. They had to try him and get it over with. The frontier was demanding; there were always jobs to be done. If a man was guilty of a crime, try him and punish him and go home and pull fodder.

The Trace was not a place to linger over a criminal. Those alive and law-abiding had enough problems without being hamstrung by violators.

It came to him with a jolt that he was thinking about his own son. That was the way it had been all afternoon: for a while Jeff would seem like his son and be very close to him, and then he would be a killer and very far away. He watched Coates give Jeff two blankets, and he and Coates turned the heavy wagon box upside down, with Jeff inside. About the only way he could escape was to dig out, and Roger asked Coates, "Has he got a knife?"

"No. I searched him."

"Will you—see that he gets some supper?"

"We'll see," said Coates. "Look, Roger, I—"

Roger shook his head. "You don't need to say it. You're doin' what you have to do. I'd do the same if it was you. Only it wouldn't be you, Virg." He looked at the wagon box and shook his head once more. "It doesn't seem like my own boy."

He hated to go home and tell Anne. They had finished supper when he got there, but he wasn't hungry. He poured a tin cup of whisky and sat down, heavy with a weariness beyond anything he had ever known. "Anne," he said.

"Yes, Roger."

He looked at her dark eyes, still soft and still alive and warm. He touched her work-worn hands. They were brown on top from the sun, and there was a big scar across the base of her left thumb where she had cut it helping him butcher. She had gone into the forest and helped him clear brush. She had plowed a furrow as straight as any of his. She could snap corn and make salt and boil molasses. She had been married at fifteen and had borne Liz before she was sixteen. All these things she had done, and brought forth five other children besides the one that had been stillborn, but her hands were still soft to the touch, well-shaped to the eye. Why did it have to happen to her?

He said, "They're going to try Jeff tomorrow for killing that boy down by Nicholson's."

Of course she had known what was coming, for she had seen strange comings and goings all day, but he saw her weave a little, and then she fell forward across his knees. He laid her gently on the bed and got the hartshorn. He held it under her nose. Her eyes opened, and she asked, "How could Jeff do a thing like that?"

"I don't know," he said.

"Do you think Jeff has been doing a lot of the things that have been happening on the Trace?"

"I don't know. He was in with a gang—a man named Setton or Taylor."

"There was a Setton escaped with Mason."

"Yes. Some said Little Harpe was with Mason too."

"Is there a connection between them?"

"Jeff's description of Setton sounds exactly like Little Harpe, the night I saw him at Knoxville."

She asked presently, "Did you have words with him at Knoxville?"

"No. Why should you ask that?"

"It almost seems as if he might have come up here and gotten Jeff into trouble to spite you."

"It doesn't sound reasonable."

"The Harpes did a lot of things that weren't reasonable, didn't they?"

"Yes, I guess they did."

That thought stayed with him. Long after Anne had silently cried herself to sleep, he was wide-eyed, staring into the dark, wondering if Little Harpe, remembering what Hughes had told him about Roger's past, was holding that over him as an unseen threat.

14 HE WAS STILL AWAKE AT SUNUP. He got quietly out of bed and into his clothes, and went to see that the stock was fed. At eight o'clock he was at Coates' place. Jeff was still under the wagon box. A short time later a dozen armed men came up the Trace and turned into the yard. Fifteen or eighteen came from above. They went off into the forest a quarter of a mile from Coates' place, and Coates set up court. "I'd rather you would elect somebody else judge of this court," he said. "The prisoner is my own kin, and I don't want to be influenced one way or another."

They elected Hiram Hall. Coates stood back of Jeff while they drew lots for jury service. Twelve men on the jury. Twelve grim, hard-faced men; men who had looked Death in the face more than once. There were few men on the Trace who hadn't lost some of their family. The Crowley baby had been killed by an alligator less than a year before. Hiram Hall himself had been of a Regulator's jury that had hung a man up near Red Banks. There wasn't much use hoping for mercy from these men, for they weren't used to receiving it. The frontier never gave odds.

And yet there was a question in Roger's mind: how much had he contributed to Jeff's lawbreaking by keeping his own past a secret? If he told that to these men, would it make any difference in Jeff's favor? Would they see that Little Harpe might have been

189

deliberately trying to get back at him? And what would they think of him, a double deserter, a damned Tory, living among them all these years in silence? What would it mean to Anne and to the rest of the children? He realized it might hurt them more than him.

He watched the jury take its place. Hall swore them in. Nicholson testified to seeing the body of the unknown, to the bullet hole in the chest, to burying the unknown. One after another they came. Practically every man there had some evidence against Jeff.

Hall didn't ask Roger to testify. He asked Jeff if he had had the blue-stocked rifle with the silver four-pointed star, and Jeff said he had. They asked him where he got it, and he said he'd taken it from the boy on the Trace.

Coates said, "He doesn't have to answer those questions if he doesn't want to."

Hall said, "No, he don't, but we'll call you and Adams to prove it."

"All right," said Coates.

The trial was over in less than an hour. Hall asked Jeff if he had anything to say, and Jeff, white and big-eyed, shook his head.

Roger stepped up. "Your honor, I would like the privilege of saying a few words on the defendant's behalf."

Hall said, "I 'low you have that right, since you're his father."

Roger paced back and forth before the jury. "Your

honor, gentlemen of the jury." He raised his head. "I ask you first to consider his age."

"How old is he?" asked a juror.

"Seventeen."

"He's old enough to know what he's doin'."

"That is true," said Roger. "I bow to the will of the jury. But I think the jury will agree that sometimes a boy of youthful years and inexperience may be led into trouble before he knows what's happening."

"That's right," said Hall.

Another juror asked, "Was there somebody else in on this killing?"

"There was."

"We better hear about it."

"Jeff fell in with a man who calls himself Setton or Taylor out in the forest. Setton first put him up to giving them information. Then he took Jeff along with him when they held up somebody, and finally they put him up to killing this boy on the Trace, and promised him that he could have the rifle."

"Where was this Setton all the time?"

"Out in the forest, waiting for his share of the booty."

"Where is he now?"

"He's still out there, for all I know."

"What does Setton look like?"

"He looks exactly like Wiley Harpe, who disappeared three years ago after his brother was killed."

"You mean Bloody Harpe?"

"One of the Bloody Harpes."

"You ever see the Harpes?" asked Hall.

"I've seen both of them."

"And you think this feller Setton is Wiley Harpe?"

"It sounds like him to me."

"If the jury figgers all you say is true, what do you think they ought to do about it?"

"I think they ought to give him a suspended sentence while I go try to catch Little Harpe."

"How do you figger to catch him?"

"He'll be around Natchez, because that's where Mason sells his stuff that he steals from flatboats. That's where Harpe would have to take the horse to sell it."

"What would happen to Jeff all this time?"

"You could keep him prisoner."

"We haven't got any money to feed a prisoner for months, maybe," said the juryman.

"I'll furnish his food."

"And we haven't got no jail," said Hall.

"I'll furnish a wagon box."

"Is that a way to live—in a wagon box?"

"It's better than dying."

Another member of the jury asked, "When do you calc'late to start this hunt for Little Harpe?"

"In the morning."

"That all you got to say?" asked Hall.

"Yes, your honor. I ask the jury to remember the prisoner's age, and to consider what I have said about Little Harpe. If it is true that one of the mad Harpes is involved in this, as I have reason to believe, I do not think a boy of this age should be made to pay the penalty by himself. I think sentence should be suspended until I either catch Little Harpe or give up."

"Jeff, you got anything to say yet?"

Jeff shook his dark, tousled head.

"You can take the prisoner back to your place, Coates, while the jury deliberates."

They went back, Jeff ahead, Coates behind, and Roger behind them both. They crossed the cornfield and came out into the yard. Anne was there. She hugged Jeff and asked Roger, "What's the verdict?"

"They're making up their minds now. I tried to get them to wait and give me a chance to bring Little Harpe for trial. I asked them to wait until I either catch him or give up."

"Will they listen to that?"

"I don't know."

"It's a pretty determined jury, ma'am," said Coates. "They saw this young feller shot down by the Trace, and they figger it's only a question of time until it'll be one of their own."

"But they should wait until the man responsible is brought to trial too, shouldn't they?"

"That was my argument," Roger said.

Liz, wet-eyed, called from the house. "I put on a meal."

"Want to eat?" Roger asked Jeff.

"I s'pose so."

Nobody said the one obvious thing—that it might be his last meal.

Liz had corn dodgers and boiled ham and potatoes and turnips and a big pan of greens. Coates poured a cup of whisky and gave it to Roger, then had one himself. "You better drink up," he told Jeff.

"I don't like it," said Jeff.

"He never did drink," said Anne.

They sat down to the puncheon table. The plates and trenchers were of wood.

"I made a Tom Fuller," Liz told Jeff. "You always liked that."

"Sure."

Roger watched him as Liz dished out the thick stew onto his plate. It was peas, corn, beans, deer meat, and nuts, shell and kernel both, but Jeff appeared not even to see it. He ate listlessly, as if he had lost interest in everything around him.

"There's watermelon for dessert," said Liz. "Will you get it, Virg? It's in the spring."

Coates brought the melon into the house. "They're still arguing up there," he said.

"Maybe that's a good sign," Anne whispered.

"Maybe. I don't know." said Roger.

And he didn't. The only thing he could seem to think of for sure now was that if he had not concealed his past, all of this might somehow not have happened.

Liz cut the melon. They each took a piece outside to eat it where they could drop the seeds on the ground.

Coates finished his melon and wiped his mouth. "They're hollerin' across the field. I reckon they've reached a decision."

Roger looked and turned cold. "They're motioning us to bring him. It doesn't look good."

Coates stared. "If they had acquitted him, they would all come down here," he said slowly.

"Jeff." Roger's voice wasn't strong, and it sounded strange to him. "Keep your backbone up, boy."

"I'll take him," said Coates. "You needn't go."

"He's my boy," said Roger. "I'll see it through."

Anne was at Roger's elbow.

"I don't think you'd best come, Anne." He tried to be gentle, but his voice seemed to crack.

She said, "He's my boy too, and I'm going to see what they do to him. Whatever they do, they'll have to do before his mother."

"The rest of you stay," Coates said, motioning Liz. She grabbed the twins and hustled them into the house.

The jury was sitting under a big oak tree when they came up. Hiram Hall was whittling out a chew. He turned the sliver of tobacco into his mouth and stuck his knife back in its sheath. "Ma'am," he said, "I'm right sorry to see you come. This is man's work."

"It is my boy," she repeated. "If it is man's work, then you are not afraid of his mother."

"No, ma'am, I reckon we're not. Prisoner, step forward and hear your sentence."

Jeff went up to Hiram Hall and faced him, smoky eyes fixed on the jury.

"The jury has reached a verdict," said Hall, and looked at Jeff. "They find the defendant guilty of murder in the first degree, and sentence him to be hung from this oak tree within an hour."

Anne swayed, and Roger caught her.

"The jury felt," Hall went on, "in spite of your argument, Roger Adams, that the defendant knew what he was doing when he pointed his rifle at the dead man's chest and pulled the trigger. He had handled a gun and he knew it would kill. He also was old enough to know it isn't right to kill a human being just to get his rifle."

"Has the jury considered—self-defense?" Roger asked.

"Far as I can see," said Hall, "there wasn't no sign of self-defense at all. The dead man wasn't bothering nobody, according to any story we've heard. You've got one hour, Jeff Adams, to get ready to meet your Maker."

Jeff sat cross-legged on the ground. Anne sat at his side, Roger at the other. Coates stood behind him.

"What about the men who were with Setton?" Roger asked Jeff. "Do you know their names?"

"There was one man named May, and two others— I forget their names. Sometimes there was a man they called John—John Mason, I think. He had been whipped at Natchez and escaped from jail."

"Anybody else?"

"I think that's all."

"Did you hear them say where the gang's headquarters might be?"

"Nothing much. They didn't talk much around me."

"Didn't they mention any towns?"

"Natchez and Hunston, I guess."

"Tell me where you found them."

"Up along the ridge toward the southwest there—anywhere, likely." Jeff seemed annoyed at being questioned.

"That's all I can do for you now," said Roger.

"What *can* you do?" asked Anne.

"I can go after them."

Anne turned pale. "I won't let you go."

Hiram Hall said, "There'll be time to eat, if anybody's hungry."

"Some of you can come to my place," said Nicholson. "I got a deer yesterday."

"The rest of you come with me," said Hall.

"Who's going to watch the prisoner?"

"He isn't going anywhere," said Roger, "but a couple of you better stick around to be sure."

"We'll take your word for him," said Hall.

"I'm not giving my word for him now."

Hall looked at Coates. "You want some help?"

"I don't think it's necessary. The kid doesn't want to get away."

Nicholson called back to Hall. "You got a rope?"

Anne sobbed.

"I said you shouldn't come," said Roger.

"I came and I'll stay," she told him, red-eyed.

Jeff pulled a few blades of grass and sucked the sweet ends.

The shadow of a hawk went across them. Roger

looked up and saw the big bough of the oak tree standing almost level with the ground, about twelve feet up.

Hall and the others came back after a while with a coil of rope. "Your time is up," he said. "I'm sorry it has to be like this, but you had plenty of time to think about that before you did it."

Jeff stood up. They tied the rope around his neck and threw the end over the bough.

"You got anything to say?" asked Hall.

Jeff shook his head.

Hall raised his arm in the signal. Jeff's slender body sprang into the air and stayed there, swinging back and forth while his smoky eyes turned dull.

In half an hour they untied the end of the rope and let the body down. Hall examined it, listened for a heart beat. Nicholson and the Duncan brothers did the same. They all looked at one another and nodded. Hall turned to Roger. "That's it," he said.

Roger picked the slender body up in his arms and carried the body down to the trail.

"I'll go with you," Coates said, "and help bury him."

They put him up on the hill by the side of Charles, and that evening, about suppertime, Roger stood looking down on the new mound of dirt.

"Something went wrong," he said. "I don't know what it was, and maybe I'll never know, but I'll get the ones that got him into this."

Later in the evening Anne came out to look for him. He was still sitting on the graveshed they had put up over Charles, his face wet, his eyes turned to the sky, where the moon was rising through the persimmons.

"It isn't right," he said. "No part of it is right."

"Don't fight it," Anne told him. "You mustn't fight it." She put one hand on his back and raised her own face to the black sky. "Sometimes," she said, "it has to happen. They can't all be good. We did what we could and raised him the best we knew how—but we don't know everything, Roger." She fell suddenly against his back, weeping. "We don't know everything."

15 HE RAN BULLETS THAT NIGHT and filled his powder horn, while Anne parched corn. He cleaned up his pistol, that he had seldom used, and put it in his belt. She filled his wallet with corn and jerked meat. He took a sack of charcoal and a tin cup, and long before sunup he was on his way down the Trace.

Hiram Hall was standing at the side of the trail just as the sky got light in the east. "I hope you don't take us wrong, Adams," he said.

"You don't expect me to like it, do you?"

"There was nothing personal in it."

"I know that," said Roger.

Hall stepped back. "I hear you're goin' after Little Harpe."

"I won't come back," Roger promised, "until his head is off the same as Big Harpe's."

He met John Swaney about half way to Natchez. "Any news about Mason or Harpe?" he asked.

"Maybe. A fellow named May came to Natchez on foot just before I left and said Mason had robbed him."

"Anything about Harpe?"

"Not especially. There's a big hunt on for both of them, and there is reward money offered, but Mason seems to be the one they want the most, because he's the one behind the gang."

He learned little in Natchez except that every man and his dog was looking for Mason and Harpe because they wanted to collect the reward money. But Mason was said to retreat across the river into Spanish Territory whenever they got too close, while nobody really knew about Harpe. Some thought he was in the country; some thought he wasn't. Mason himself was said to have laughed at the idea of Harpe's being in his gang. But there were others who remembered how Little Harpe had disappeared from Kentucky, and they pointed out it was not likely he would take to honest ways after the life he had led, so what better place could he find to hide than Mason's gang?

Roger saw Governor Claiborne and talked it over with him. Claiborne said yes, there was reward money, but it wasn't making Mason any easier to find. He gave Roger a glass of peach brandy and said, "What do I know about Harpe? Nothing, really, except that men who have seen him up in Kentucky claim to have seen him along the Trace. Reports from New Orleans indicate that he and Sefton and Taylor are all one and the same man. I believe he has used the names of Roberts and Wells also. The thing is, the man is a mad dog. Whatever name he travels by, we've got to get him or he'll disrupt the entire government in Mississippi Territory."

"He's one who has to be stopped, all right."

"Have you ever seen him?" asked Claiborne.

"Yes."

"Do you remember the color of his hair?"

"Red," said Roger. "Sometimes they called him Red-Haired Harpe."

"Some say he was black-haired."

"His brother, Big Harpe, was black-haired. Not this one."

"What else do you remember about his looks?"

Roger recalled Jeff's description, and said grimly, "He had a scowly, evil countenance—and yet it didn't seem evil to everybody. Sometimes they posed as preachers and got by very nicely. It is said they could make a prayer or give a blessing that was a credit to any preacher in the West."

Claiborne filled his glass again. "Then they aren't just killers alone. That is, some say they kill without reason."

"That seems to have been true in Kentucky—but not so down here. My own feeling is that Little Harpe was the brains of the two. He's just as bloody, but he's smart. How else could he keep away from the law for so long?"

Claiborne smiled wryly. "Admittedly there isn't too much law down here—but it does seem, if he were as stupid as some believe, he would have fallen afoul of somebody sooner or later. He's been on the loose for a long time now."

"Too long," said Roger.

Claiborne looked at him curiously. "You're a leading man in the territory South of Tennessee, aren't you?"

"Not necessarily leading. I'm one of the oldest settlers."

"How old?"

"I came in right after the war, as soon as the United States occupied this part of the country. There were still Spanish soldiers here."

"There are a few yet," Claiborne said, "but we tolerate them. We're not ready to make an issue of it. The time is coming, however. The Kentucky Country is overflowing, and something will have to be done. We are trying to give the Spanish a chance to withdraw their troops gracefully. They are nothing more than token forces anyway, now that the United States has bought Louisiana. But what I started to ask you is, how would you people up around the bend of the Tennessee River feel about coming into Mississippi Territory?"

"We haven't considered that so much. There is some talk that we have to have an organized government. We're too far from North Carolina."

"I think North Carolina and Georgia will soon cede their claims to the government, and then there will be the question of what to do with your territory. It is really too small to make a state."

"We could join onto Tennessee."

"Yes, of course. More brandy? However, Tennessee is already a good-sized state in its own right. Personally, I'd like to see you become a part of Mississippi Territory. This area is somewhat small."

Roger put down his glass. "I could ask around and let you know—soon as I get back."

"When do you expect to be back?"

"Soon as I catch Little Harpe."

Claiborne eyed him. "Something personal?"

"You might call it that."

"By the way, Mr. Adams—if you don't mind my saying so, you talk rather well for a settler. I take it you've had more education than some."

"Yes."

Claiborne eyed him but said no more.

Roger went out through the swamps and the bayous and walked the chestnut through the ancient forests. Under oaks and sycamores alike he stopped to observe and to listen. He heard the crows around the cornfields during the day, and at night he listened to the rising hum of mosquitoes, to bullfrogs and alligators, and once in a while, deep in the forest, he would see the fast vanishing Mississippi tiger—but only for an instant.

Not even for that long did he lay eyes on Mason or Little Harpe. He talked to settlers in the country; he killed game when he was close to a cabin. He asked innumerable questions and got as many answers. If he hadn't seen Little Harpe up in Kentucky, he would have thought the man a myth.

He made headquarters in Natchez and searched the country northeast and northwest of that town for the cave that Mason was reported to occupy. He found a number of caves. Most of them had been used—some obviously by a large number of men—and he found some of them occupied by hunters or trappers, but there was no indication of Harpe or Mason.

He ran into other men hunting the outlaws; most of the pursuers traveled in packs, and their trails crisscrossed among the swamps and bayous until it seemed not a living soul could have escaped notice. Eventually Roger went across the river to Fort Concordia, in Spanish territory, but he hadn't a chance there. Yellow-coated soldiers watched the river crossings like hawks, and wasted no time turning him back. It was obvious, then, that if Mason at times retreated across the river, he used some other place to cross.

In late October Roger returned to Natchez. In that time he had no word from home, and he sat down in his room to write Anne a letter. It was short because there was little to tell.

"I have not found Harpe yet. There are many reports but he is hard to track down. I shall keep on trying. The man cannot evade the whole countryside forever. My best love to you and the children, Virgil and Liz and the twins."

Thinking of Anne, he felt a disinclination to stay down in the Natchez country on a project that seemed so ephemeral, but this matter between Harpe and him had to be cleared up. Harpe was the man who knew his secret. Harpe! He thought no further. You couldn't kill a man in cold blood because he knew a secret about you. But was Harpe a man? Was he entitled to the consideration of a man, or was he rather some kind of dangerous animal to be shot down at the first opportunity? Roger mulled over that question quite a while, and finally he went down the steep path to

Natchez-Under-the-Hill, the narrow shelf lined with saloons, houses of prostitution, and a few legitimate businesses. Down there flatboats docked—those that got by Cave-in-Rock and Diamond Island and Hurricane Bar and the snags and sawyers, floating islands and falling banks, Indians and white pirates.

They pulled in to Natchez-Under-the-Hill to get warmed up for New-Orleans, the city of sin, to find women (they invariably had plenty of whisky), and to fight. Occasionally, too, sailing vessels came up the river from New Orleans and anchored out in the middle of the half-mile channel and sent goods in by canoe and skiff. Men of many nationalities, without women for a long time, added up to violence of many kinds. They were, of course, careless with money—and Natchez-Under-the-Hill was designed to get all the loose money possible as easily as possible. It was not a place to inspire confidence, but Roger went down there for information.

He walked into the Boatman's Bar, a noisy, smoky, stale-smelling place. A skimpily dressed girl sitting on the bar, with her bare legs showing up to her thighs, looked at him and started to jump down. He shook his head at her and went on past. He threw out a pie-shaped two-bit piece and said, "Spirits."

The bartender poured a small glass of whisky; he let the money and the bottle stay on the bar. Roger poured another. The bartender came back and scooped up the two-bit piece and started off. Roger said, "Hold up a minute."

The bartender turned back. He leaned one hairy arm on the rough pine and said, "What'll it be?"

Roger threw out another piece of a coin and poured a third. He said, "Where's Anthony Glass?"

The bartender didn't move and his expression didn't change. "Never heard of him."

"I understand he handles some goods for Samuel Mason."

"That's not my line," said the bartender, keeping one hairy arm on the counter.

"What if a man had some stuff to sell— cheap?"

"You could try Glass. I don't know."

"Where is he?"

"Warehouse on the dock, right across from here. You must of been blind or you'd of seen it; 'Anthony Glass, Merchant'."

"Maybe my eyes aren't as good as they might be."

"Maybe not. Pour a fourth. I can't break that."

"I'm not ready for a fourth. Keep the change."

The two-bit piece disappeared in the bartender's vest pocket. "All right, mister."

He pushed outside through the blue swinging half-doors. Almost directly across, at the edge of the water, was a big building, and on top was the sign. He saw a door at the corner, with a small window at one side. He let a party of drunken flatboatmen go by, then went across and pushed open the door. A man looked up from a small table he was using as a desk. He was sitting so that he faced the door, and Roger knew it was no accident. He was a very fat man, but his eyes were black and sharp, deep in his face. A pistol seemed to be holding down some papers, but Roger had the feeling that it had other functions.

"Who are you?" asked the fat man.

"I'm Roger Adams from the territory South of Tennessee."

Glass looked at him. "All right, what do you want?"

"I'm looking for a man known as Setton, who used to be with Mason."

Glass sat back. "So are a lot of others. Why come to me? Why don't you get out and hunt for him?"

"I understand that Setton used to be with Mason."

"It is hard to know things like that."

"I understand that you once testified against Setton in favor of Mason."

Glass picked up the quill. "Setton was one of a party who robbed a boat owned by me and a man named Owsley. Setton testified at New Madrid that Mason had committed this robbery, and I merely wished to correct that statement."

"Why did you care what happened to Mason?"

"I had had business with Sam Mason, and he had always treated me fairly."

"You mean he sold you at half price the goods he took from men he murdered."

Glass laid down the pen. "You're on dangerous ground, mister."

"If you make a move toward that pistol," Roger said, "I'll have you by the throat."

Glass looked at the pistol and then at Roger, and dropped his hands in his lap. "Say what you want to say and then get out."

"I want to know where to look for Setton."

"I don't do business with Setton."

"I understand that your wife's brother was also mixed up in some robberies, and you were afraid to turn in Setton for fear he would talk."

Glass's black eyes did not change. "My wife's brother takes care of his own affairs. Besides, nothing that Setton could say against him would hurt. Setton is a deserter."

"What difference does that make?"

"The word of a man who is a deserter from the army has no legal bearing. Furthermore, if he falls into the hands of military authorities he will be immediately arrested and held for court-martial."

Roger thought about that for a long time. Finally he said, "Setton's acts are making it difficult for Mason to operate."

"I live," Glass said in a bored tone. "Boats come to Natchez and want to sell out cheap. I buy. Mason is no concern of mine."

"A minute ago you said he was your friend."

Glass's eyes became tiny in his fat face. "What do you want?" he asked again.

"To find Setton."

"You might not want him after you find him."

"I'll take that chance."

Glass waved his fat arm. "Anywhere in the Natchez

area. Setton is a man hard to locate. He might be under your nose at this very minute."

Roger looked at him. Glass was telling him where to find Little Harpe!

He backed out and closed the door. He went back across the street. Down here somewhere, at Natchez-Under-the Hill, Setton might be expected tonight.

Roger started at the Green Parrot, to the right of the Boatmen's Bar. He had a drink, looked around, listened to the tinny piano and the metallic-sounding banjo, looked at the women with laughing faces but cold eyes, and went on. He went down to the end, where Indians and Negroes were drinking, and there the women were bolder.

A quadroon girl stood beside him. "Buy me a drink?" she asked.

He looked at her. She was beautiful, as most quadroons were beautiful, with olive brown skin, lustrous eyes, red lips, and white teeth. And she was only about sixteen.

He bought her a drink. "You want to sleep with me tonight?" she asked.

He looked at her and swallowed. "Not enough," he said finally.

She tossed her head to one side and backed a step swinging her hips from side to side. "You are not a man for a place like this, but if you want a woman, I will stay with you all night for two pesetas."

"I'm sorry," he said. "I'm here on business. I'll buy you another drink."

She took it. "You are a man, aren't you?"

He looked at her casually and nodded. He didn't say that she was probably vermin-ridden or diseased. He said instead, "I'm here on business—that has to be finished tonight."

She teased. "What is such important business?"

"I'm looking for a man." He laid two pesetas on the counter. "For that much money you would stay with me all night."

"Not for the money alone," she said, looking at him boldly.

"I've got to find a certain man. I will give you the two pesetas to help me."

For a moment she sulked. Then a calculating gleam appeared in her lustrous eyes. She picked up the money and dropped it inside the front of her dress, and it was impossible to avoid noticing her large and handsome breasts. She let him stare, and then asked, "So who is this man you want to find?"

"John Setton."

She hesitated for an instant. "Setton? He's a madman—a killer. Are you sure?"

"I'm sure."

She drew near. "Go to the Boatmen's Bar. He's there now."

He strode out. It was still only midafternoon, but the clouds were gathering in the southwest and he thought it would be a cold rain. He went back to the Boatmen's Bar and pushed through the shutter doors. He ordered spirits. He drank it. Then he allowed himself to look around the smoky room.

It did not take long. At the other end of the bar stood two men. One was a heavy-set man, a little under average height, with a scowly face and red, wavy hair that came down almost to his eyebrows—Wiley Harpe.

16 ROGER'S PISTOL WAS IN HIS BELT. He could feel his tomahawk against his right hip and his knife at his left. He picked up his change and started toward Harpe.

At that moment another man came in the back door and started for the front. He had a star on his shirt and a rifle in his hand. Roger stopped.

The new man obviously was looking for somebody. His gaze swept the room as he half-turned not stopping his forward progress.

Harpe was back in the corner formed by the end of the bar and the wall of a small room that projected into the big room. If the man from the back door was looking for Harpe he didn't see him. On second thought, Roger realized he had no reason to think the man was looking for Harpe.

The man looked sharply at Roger but strode on by. He went through the swinging half-doors without looking around. Roger finished his drink and moved down the bar.

"You're Wiley Harpe," he said.

Harpe was drunk but there was no mistaking his dangerousness. He had two pistols in his belt and the usual tomahawk at his right hip. He was bareheaded, and his red hair came low on his forehead. He looked at Roger, a little bleary-eyed, but Roger knew the automatic functions of that killing mind were as alert as ever.

"I'm Setton." His words were a little thick. "John Setton."

Roger made sure his right hand was free. "You're Harpe," he said. "I saw you in Knoxville in '98."

Harpe's eyes almost closed. He weaved a little, and said, "I can tell you who you are too. You're Robert Ashby, and you served with Tarleton, and—" He stopped.

Roger stared for an instant. For a long time he had foreseen this and dreaded it. Now it had come. He had been accused. At this long last it was a relief to hear it finally come into the open. And this was the man who had led Jeff into a killing. Roger's hand went for his tomahawk.

But a voice behind him said over his shoulder, "You're Setton, eh?"

The man with the star was there. Roger took a step back to get out of range.

But Setton was not altogether a fool. He looked at the man. His head wavered, but his eyes fastened on the star.

"Setton—that's my name."

"I'm sheriff here."

"There ain't no sheriff here."

The man at Setton's side began to back away.

"Maybe you didn't hear me. I said I'm sheriff in Natchez."

Setton seemed to think it over. He looked at the pistol in the sheriff's belt. "What do you want?" he asked.

"Who's this with you?"

The second man stopped edging away. "I'm James May."

"Fine! I'm lookin' for you too!"

Setton began to stall. "What do you want us for?"

"You two robbed a man named Winters, up near Hunston. I'm arresting you."

"Now, hold on, sheriff," said Harpe, and Roger could see the man's crafty brain working in his eyes. "Would you rather have two small-sized fish like us or one big one like Samuel Mason?"

"What's that got to do with it?"

"We're on our way to get Mason."

There was silence for a moment. Then the sheriff said, "Ev'rybody in the country is lookin' for Mason. How can you find him any quicker than anybody else?"

I know where he is," said Harpe. "I was with Mason when he escaped from the Spanish. I know where his headquarters are— —over in Spanish territory."

"That doesn't say you can get close to him."

"I was with Mason for half a year. I was with him when he was arrested at Little Prairie. Sure, he'll let me within gunshot of him."

"What about you, May?"

"Mason held me up," said the man at Harpe's side. "Don't you think I want to get even?"

There was a circle of men and women around them now. "Sure, sheriff," said a big man in a Spanish hat, "these here fellers are small time. Turn 'em loose and let 'em bring in Mason if they can."

"Who guarantees they'll come back?"

"Five hundred dollars reward will bring 'em back if they get Mason."

The sheriff was a little stubborn. "But these here fellers robbed a man too."

"Mason has robbed a thousand men—and killed a hundred. You can afford to gamble on two small fellers like this to get your hands on one big one."

Setton looked at Roger then, and Roger thought he was about to speak. Roger's hand went to his tomahawk and he stared back at the man. The sheriff looked at Setton. "Maybe Mason won't be easy to take alive."

"We'll bring you his head," said Setton. "It's easier than bringin' back the man's body anyway."

The sheriff said, "As far as the Territory of Mississippi is concerned, there's no denying we'd rather have Mason than you. The governor told me that himself. Not that the governor likes you," he said emphatically, "but Mason has got a big gang and we've got to break it up. I'm half a mind to make a deal with you."

"What's the deal?" asked Harpe.

"I'll turn you loose to get Mason. If you get him I'll ask the judge to go easy on you. But if you don't come back here in a week," he warned, "I'll be after you with a pack of bloodhounds, and I'll put your head up on the Natchez Trace."

Harpe raised his glass. "A week is lots of time, sheriff. We'll be back after the reward money."

Roger kept back. He wanted just one thing—to keep

an eye on Setton—or Harpe, whichever you wanted to call him.

An hour later Setton and May left the Boatmen's Bar and walked unsteadily down the planks along the river. Roger followed at a distance. It had begun to rain, and it was as dark as after sundown. He saw Setton and May get into a canoe and start across the Mississippi. He watched them until they disappeared in the gloom. Then he found another canoe, bought it from a Choctaw Indian, and set out across the river himself. If the river should come up enough to overflow its high banks and flood the swampland, especially on the west side, tracking would be difficult, but the water was comparatively low, and it was not likely that it would rain enough to bring the river up. Therefore the men would be easy to track.

He rowed straight across the water and pulled his canoe up on the sand. He walked downstream until he found recent similar marks. He went back into the willows and found the canoe the two men had used. He hid his own canoe and took up the trail.

The two men had skirted Fort Concordia which had a small Spanish garrison. Then they went down into swampy county. Roger followed their trail as far as he could before dark. Then he stopped to make camp in a cold, drizzling rain that made the sycamores look like gaunt gray ghosts in the semi-darkness, and the moss hanging from tree limbs like velvet-heavy garments looping for ethereal arms. He wrapped his wallet around the breech of his rifle to protect the charge, and laid it at his side. He dug a hole in the black dirt and built a small fire of charcoal in the hole, so it would not show a flame above the ground. Then he sat with his legs crossed the heat coming up between them. He wrapped his single blanket around him to cover his back and the fire too, and there, warm and quite invisible from ten feet away, he sat through the night, occasionally chewing parched corn or jerked venison, catching rain water on the brim of his hat to drink, watching the impenetrable darkness, listening to the croaking of bullfrogs, an occasional splash as a big alligator lumbered into the water. Here there were no coyotes or wolves; those would be on higher ground. Here there were only the noises of the swamp world, the weird blue-yellow luminance of fireflies as they winged along waist high. The swamp was filled with life of many kinds, and his ears, his eyes, and his nose strained to separate the evidence offered. The rain stopped, but mosquitoes did not bother him because of the heat arising from the blanket, for which he was grateful. Though he might have to stay awake all night, for he did not know how far behind the two men he was, he would be warm, and unmolested by the insects, which, judging by their sound, were hovering over the swamp in clouds.

Presently, however, he smelled meat cooking, and located the fire by the reflected glow from the low-hanging clouds. They were not over a quarter of a mile away, and he watched their fire for a long time, until he was sure they had allowed it to go out by itself.

From time to time he heard their voices, although human sound did not carry too well through swamp vegetation. And finally, when he felt sure they were settled for the night, he dozed.

He was brought up sharply by their voices again. His fire was out. It had quit raining, and he prepared to travel, remembering that he had a number of things to watch for: Mason and his gang, Setton and May, and the Spanish soldiers—for he was in alien country without a passport. From the freedom with which Setton and May moved about, it did not seem likely that he would encounter trouble with the Spanish. He arose, folded his blanket, threw his wallet over his shoulder, and sat behind a sycamore tree chewing parched corn while Setton and May prepared break-fast. He watched a cottonmouth moccasin slide off into the muddy water as the sun came up. Shortly after, Setton and May were on the move. Setton seemed to know where he was going, and led the way. May followed. Roger followed them both at a distance.

This went on all day. Toward evening he expected the two men to stop to camp, but they did not—which he took to be an indication that they were nearing Mason's headquarters. Setton was still threading his way through the swamp. They stopped for a rest. Roger stayed in a grove of swamp oak, out of their sight, and watched them eat some jerked meat, heard their unguarded voices. He tried to make out what they were saying, but suddenly, in his intentness, he heard the sound behind him on a foot pulled out of sucking mud!

He dropped to the ground, rolled over to a big sycamore, came to his feet on the far side. He waited, tense, a quarter of an hour, but there was no other sound. Somebody had been trailing him. Why? No sheriff would be doing it. No United States sheriff would be in Spanish country. Spanish soldiers would not be so secretive. They come tramping along, depending on numbers for safety. Then what? There was only one reasonable answer: a guard for Mason.

Roger wondered how long the man had been trailing him. He was hidden behind the trunk of the tree, watching his backtrail from over the crotch of a limb. The man behind would have to move soon or lose Setton and May. Roger stood motionless.

Finally he saw a tall half-breed with a Mexican straw hat move out of a clump of reeds. The man walked noiselessly on moccasins, peering in all directions, a rifle in his left hand, the haft of a big-bladed knife in his other. He must have stepped unwittingly into a pothole to make that sucking noise.

He passed the sycamore. Roger moved around the big trunk slowly, gauging his position by the speed of the half-breed's progress, careful not to step on the flowing roots of the tree for fear they would creak.

The breed went past him, and Roger paused a moment to consider his next move. He wanted to be sure Setton did not get away. If Setton were trying to escape from American justice, he would take him back to face it, for he had many scores to settle with Little Harpe.

Roger called on all his hard-learned memories of Indian fighting. He kept back, behind the trees, far out of hearing, watching the half-breed trail the two ahead. But they were not as close to Mason as he had thought. That night they camped on a dry piece of ground, with the breed staying back in the dark, and Roger trying to keep the breed in sight.

It was noon the next day when the breed finally readied his rifle and drew a bead on one of the two men, by which Roger judged they were finally getting close to Mason's camp. Roger considered that for the space of a few seconds. For some reason the breed was not worrying about Roger's whereabouts. Maybe he thought Roger had been in Setton's party.

Up ahead, Setton was moving around, and the breed's rifle moved also. Roger slid up quietly, with his knife in his hand. He pressed the sharp point through the buckskin of the breed's hunting shirt. He said no word, but the breed first tensed, then relaxed. The rifle came down. He turned around slowly. Roger had his pistol in his left hand. He motioned the man to lay the rifle on the ground, intending to tie him up, for he wanted Setton and May to get Mason if they could.

The breed's knife was in its sheath. Roger watched sharply, as he laid down the rifle. The breed straightened up suddenly, and his knife was in his hand, but not soon enough.

Roger's long blade sank through his hunting shirt

and into his chest, and Roger's left hand was up high as he brought down the pistol on top of the breed's head to keep him from yelling.

The breed sank, the weight of his body pulling itself free of Roger's knife. The man was dead. Roger straightened him out and looked for Setton and May. They were eating.

They moved on presently, and Roger followed. They reached a small stream with banks of blue clay, and Setton led the way up the middle of the bed.

In the middle of the afternoon they arrived at a large camp, where saddles, bridles, clothing, and other pieces of equipment lay scattered on the ground. Roger judged that at times there were twenty-five or thirty men there, but at this time there seemed to be only one—a large, portly older man who obviously was Samuel Mason.

Roger found cover in a wild plum thicket. It was too far for him to hear what they said, but he had to stay in hiding. Men might come in at any time for a raid, and he did not dare to be caught again from the rear. He had been lucky the first time. He couldn't count on that again.

Mason seemed glad to see Setton and offered him a drink from a demijohn. Presently he let down a quarter of venison from a tree, and Setton sliced it up and put the steaks on rocks to broil.

By now it was getting dark. Roger had moved away from the stream, which probably was the main line of travel, and had taken up a position behind a pecan tree on the opposite side of the camp, considerably puzzled as to just what he could or should do. If Mason's gang should return, he would have to withdraw to some distance to avoid discovery.

But more important was Setton's objective. If he really intended to kill Mason, then undoubtedly he would go back to Natchez to get the reward. If he had used the chase after Mason as an excuse to get away, then Roger would have to figure out a plan to get Setton away from the camp and start him back to Natchez.

The problem was solved by Setton. Perhaps they were fortunate to have come at a time when Mason was alone. Perhaps Setton had known he would be alone. At any rate, they ate together, drank from the demijohn, and old Mason obviously was in a good mood. He talked and laughed and sometimes roared, slapping Setton on the back. Roger kept moving and watching behind him. He did not want a steel blade in his back.

It grew dark, but Roger could see them by the light of the campfire. The hum of mosquitoes arose from the swampy ground. A bobcat howled. A wild turkey thundered off across the swamp.

Mason now lay almost prone, his head on a saddle, drinking from the demijohn. Setton finally looked up at May and nodded. May moved around behind Mason. He kicked the saddle from under the man's head. Mason turned on his side to protest, and Setton buried his tomahawk in the big man's skull.

Roger watched as they cut around the man's head. They finished by twisting it off, just as Steigal had done with Big Harpe's. They took the head down to the stream, and Setton dug up handful after handful of the blue clay and packed the gory head, now pretty well-drained of blood. Then, becoming wary again, they slipped back down the stream bed the way they had come. Obviously they intended to get out of sight as soon as possible.

They traveled all night, taking turns carrying the head. Roger followed at a safe distance, depending largely on the sounds of their progress, partly on his memory of the path over which they had come. His only fear now was that somebody else would intercept them.

For two clays and nights they traveled steadily. The men up ahead seemed tireless. Again they skirted the fort. They reached the river bank and followed it until they came to their canoe. They put the canoe in the water, loaded the head in the bow, and set out across the river.

It was early morning, the river was covered with fog—but fog could lift. Roger waited until they had time to get across. Then he found his own canoe and crossed higher up the river.

17 WHEN HE REACHED NATCHEZ-UNDER-THE-HILL and went in for a drink at the Boatmen's Bar, there was considerable excitement in the saloon. "Them two fellers come in here with Sam Mason's head under their arm!"

"Where did they take it?" asked Roger, paying for his drink.

"Up on the hill to get the reward."

A backwoodsman said, "Ah, there weren't no head in there. Sam Mason's too slick a cuss to be taken in by them two."

The bartender shrugged. "It's not my money."

Roger finished his drink and went out. He climbed the hill and inquired the news. Everybody was talking about the two men who had Sam Mason's head in blue clay. They had gone to the circuit judge, they said, to show the head and to make an affidavit so as to claim the reward money from Governor Claiborne.

Roger was directed to the courthouse, in a red brick building with a blue tiled roof. He went inside. The room was jammed with men, but Roger pushed through. Up in froth was a flat table, and facing it, with their backs to the room, were Setton and May. Setton had the lump of blue clay under his arm.

On the opposite side of the table sat a fat man with a goatee.

Roger got close enough to hear what was said.

"You claim the reward for capturing Samuel Mason?"

"We claim the money," said Setton.

"Where *is* Mason?"

"His body is across the river, past Fort Concordia."

The fat man had a nasal Yankee drawl. "How can I certify that you are entitled to the money if he is dead?"

"The poster said dead or alive."

The fat man had a shrewd look. "How can I know if he's dead. You might have killed somebody else."

John Setton placed the big ball of blue clay in the center of the table. "We brung his head," he said.

The fat man pushed his chair back abruptly. He looked at the ball of clay and back at Setton. Finally his judicial mind took hold. "How do I know it's Mason's head?"

Setton's tomahawk was out. There was absolute stillness in the room. Setton cracked the hard clay with the back of the tomahawk. He picked off a piece of the shell and tossed it on the floor, where it shattered with a sharp, small tinkling sound. Setton took off another piece, and the dead man's nose was revealed. Setton used the tomahawk again, and picked off more pieces, and a moment later the floor was littered with clay, while the ghastly white benevolence of old Mason's face was revealed in full.

There was still a breathless silence. The fat man got up and walked around the table to look at the face. He touched the head gingerly and then backed away. Finally he looked at Setton. "When did this happen?" he asked.

There was a general intake of breath among the watchers. It was a head, a human head, and not many days ago it had been attached to a man. It wasn't now.

Setton said, "We killed him three days ago."

"The head is not—has not putrefied."

"It's cool weather. Any kind of game will keep in this weather," said Setton without emotion.

The judge visibly repressed a shudder.

"The clay kept the air away from it."

The judge looked at the crowd. "Can anybody identify this—this man?"

A lanky boatman at Roger's side spoke up. "That's Mason, all right. I was on a flatboat held up by him last spring. He came aboard, and I had a good look at him."

"Is there any feature about him that—"

The man moved a long arm against Roger's side. "That tooth," he said. "It reminded me of a wolf's fang, and he was always trying to keep his lip over it. I'd know that anywhere." He turned to Roger. "Wouldn't you?"

Roger thought of many things. He remembered Big Harpe's head nailed up at Robertson's Lick. He looked at the gruesome head with its projecting tooth, probably now more accentuated because of the shrinking flesh. It gave the face an animal-like caricature that made a man shudder. He looked at Setton again and wondered how long it would be before that man's head was on a post by the side of the road. Finally he looked back at the boatman. "If I'd ever seen it," he said, "I think I'd remember it."

"He held me up on the Trace this summer," said another. "He said his name was Mason."

"Anybody could say their name was Mason," the judge pointed out. "I will have to have better identification than that. Mason's wife lives near Shankstown. Perhaps—"

Setton said dangerously, "Hasn't the Territory got the money to pay the reward?"

The judge said, "The Territory's funds are not large. We can pay the reward, but we must have assurance this is the man. I will get in touch with the governor at once."

"When do we know?" Setton asked sullenly.

"By dinnertime. Come back then. And—er—leave the head. We may be able to get identification in other ways."

"You'll have to scrub your table, jedge," said a man in the back.

"That thing won't be very sweet-smelling by dinnertime," said another.

"I shall make every effort," the judge assured them, "to secure identification. In the meantime," he told Setton and May, "hold yourselves available. I know the sheriff made a deal with you, but the deal is of no effect unless this is Mason's head."

Roger stayed in the background. He himself had no

absolute knowledge that this was Mason's head, he thought as he had a drink at the tavern. He was tired, having been almost without sleep for four or five nights, and the spirits made him sleepy. He sat at a table and nodded, awakening when someone came in and announced to the room, "Gov'nor Claiborne has sent his carriage for Mrs. Mason!"

Roger got up and went back to the courthouse. The large crowd outside was eager to dispense information. "Sure, he's been identified by a dozen men. What are they waiting on? Can't the governor pay the reward he offered?"

A fine carriage rolled up, drawn by two blooded red roans. A Negro footman opened the door, and a heavily-veiled woman stepped down. She went inside, and Roger was in the crowd that followed her. She walked straight to the table, stared at the head lying on its side, and spoke to the fat judge. "That is not my husband's head."

The judge thought it over. "You're sure of this, Mrs. Mason?"

"Absolutely."

The judge sighed. "You will pardon me, madam. I had hoped your answer would be otherwise."

"I know my husband," she said, and turned and swept from the room, elegant, even regal, in her heavy silk dress that swept the floor.

The fat judge looked at Setton and May. "This represents something of a dilemma. If the man's own wife refuses to identify him—"

"Judge," said John May, "I know Mason. I was held up by him, last spring."

"You were held up," the judge said. "How could you be positive that Mason did it?"

"They called him Mason."

"That may have been deliberate. They could have agreed to call anybody Mason for the purpose of creating an illusion."

May turned away obviously disgusted, but Setton said ominously, "We risked our lives to bring in this man's head. Aren't we going to get our money?"

"I'm not questioning your bravery or the obvious fact that you have brought in a head. The only question that concerns me is whose head is it?"

"I can answer that," Setton said abruptly. "I know Mason as well as any man alive."

The judge looked at him shrewdly. "How?"

Setton put both hands on the table. "If I turn state's evidence," he said, "will I be guaranteed against prosecution?"

The judge put his fingertips together and said slowly, "If you have been connected with Mason, and if you are willing to testify against him and his gang, I think I can promise you immunity from prosecution for crimes committed in that connection."

Setton said in a low voice, "I was a member of Mason's gang when he was arrested at Little Prairie. I had been with him about a month then."

"And your name is—"

"John Setton."

The judge murmured, "We do not have the records of the inquiry at Little Prairie, and there is no immediate way of checking those facts."

"My name is on the records. My testimony was taken down. Mason tried to blame me for everything he had done. I was taken to New Orleans with him, and we were sent back up the river to Natchez, but escaped."

"How long did you stay with him, then?"

"Long enough to find out where he would hide out, for I had sworn to get even." Setton's voice was filled with venom.

"I understand his first hideout was at Rocky Springs, on this side of the river."

"He had two places. If they got too close to him at Rocky Springs, he went across the river beyond the fort."

"That sounds like Mason," said a voice. "He always did work on both sides."

The judge appeared to speculate. "Come back this afternoon," he said finally, "and I will give you my decision."

Setton grumbled and May looked disgusted, but there was nothing they could do. They had to have a certificate from the judge before they could call on the governor for the money.

The crowd thinned slowly, and Roger Adams, filling up on hog and hominy, considered his own situation. He had come after Harpe, and Mason was none of his business, nor was the reward money any affair of his. Only Harpe concerned him; he was determined to take

Harpe back up the Trace to be tried by the same jury that had tried Jeff. In the meantime, apparently no one suspected that Setton was Harpe, even though there was a four-hundred dollar reward on Harpe's head too. The man had gall to bring in another man's head and insist on the reward money, when his own head rested so lightly on his thick shoulders.

There was another factor. He knew that Setton was Harpe, and Harpe knew he knew it. Harpe also knew that Roger Adams was Robert Ashby. Nobody had noticed that in the Boatmen's Bar—but what now? Sometime, some place, all this knowledge would have to erupt.

He was finishing his coffee when a man appeared in the door and announced dramatically, "They're goin' to get the certificate!"

Roger got up and paid for his meal. He crowded out with the rest of them, and the mass of men, filling the street and gathering others as it went along, headed for the judge's courtroom. Roger got inside. The judge was saying, "Now you have both sworn under oath that this is the head of Samuel Mason, and that you have qualified for the reward money. Sign here or put your X's and we will get witnesses to them."

May marked a big "X," and a scrawny man volunteered eagerly to witness it. He got ink on the quill pen and laboriously wrote his name. Setton signed his own name at the bottom, "John Setton." The judge took the pen and began to write out the certificate on a large sheet of heavy paper.

There was a commotion in the back of the room, and a tall, leather-faced man in a linsey-woolsey hunting shirt pushed through. He scrutinized both Setton and May, and turned to the judge. "Arrest both of these men!" he said. "They held me up on the Trace and killed the man with me!"

The judge stopped writing. He looked at the tall man and then at Setton. He looked at the certificate, then put the pen in its holder and leaned back.

Setton turned slowly and scowled at the big man. Some vehement emotion was working in his brain. "I've never seen you before," he said heatedly, "and I've never been on the Trace. I was with Mason across the river."

"You ain't foolin' me," the man said. "I'd know that scowly face of yourn anywhere. I reco'nized your horses in the stable—both of 'em blaze-faced."

Setton's hand went to his tomahawk, but the man didn't back water. He said again to the judge, "Arrest these two, your honor!"

The judge sighed. "One thing at a time, I'm afraid. The sheriff is the man to see if you want them arrested. I am concerned now with deciding whether this head is the head of Samuel Mason."

The leather-faced man gaped. Then he leaned over the table. "You mean you won't arrest these men?"

"I have no authority to arrest. See the sheriff next door. There is plenty of time. These men will have to go to the governor to get their money."

Setton glared at the leather-faced man; a cold look

was in his eyes. The leather-faced man turned on his heel, muttering, "Talk about justice!"

The judge finished writing the certificate and signed it. He sprinkled sand on the paper and held it up, hitting it against the table top to jar the sand loose. He handed the certificate, on heavy paper, to Setton. "Take this to the governor's house up the hill, and he will give you the money. For your sake, I hope you are not guilty of the murder you are accused of."

"We ain't been on the Trace at all," Setton said belligerently. He took the certificate and went out through the crowd, which moved after him.

Roger thought the end was in sight and he knew now what he would do. Setton and May could not go back across the river. They'd spend the reward money in Natchez and then set out to rob travelers on the Trace. When they did, Roger would be behind them. When he got an opportunity he would take them captive, alive if possible, dead if necessary.

He followed them to the governor's house. The entire crowd, consisting now of over a hundred men, tried to crowd up on the front porch behind Setton and May.

A Negro butler came to the door. He spoke to Setton in a low voice and then said, "If you-all'll wait heah, suh, ah'll fetch the gov'nor."

They waited. Claiborne appeared, a medium tall, youngish man with a Napoleon forelock. He looked at the certificate and then at Setton and May. A man appeared in the doorway behind him. This was an older man, dressed in the usual buckskin hunting shirt. The governor, still examining the certificate, said pleasantly, "Gentlemen, this is Captain Stump, who has come here in command of a company to aid the United States to take possession of Louisiana. Captain Stump is an old Indian fighter from the Kentucky Country."

There was no comment. The governor apparently finished perusing the certificate, and said to Setton, "If you will return in an hour, your check will be ready."

Setton glowered, but there was little he could do. He turned, with May behind him, and went through the crowd, which opened for him as before.

Roger had been at one side, and this left him far in the rear. Everybody else was off of the porch when he heard Captain Stump say, "That man Setton looks like Wiley Harpe!"

Claiborne answered, "Surely not. He wouldn't have the nerve to come here to collect reward money for Mason if he were Harpe."

"When it's Harpe," Stump said, "anything goes."

"Harpe is said to have been killed at Cave-in-Rock."

"Maybe Setton himself told that. I'll swear Setton is a dead ringer for Harpe."

"Have you seen Harpe?"

"I knew him in Knoxville."

Claiborne said thoughtfully, "If he is, we'll nail him when he comes back."

"He may not come back."

Claiborne smiled. "Setton doesn't know it," he

said, "but he has been followed by a deputy ever since he got back with that head. If he is Harpe, he'll hang!"

Roger drew away slowly and thought that over for the next hour as he coddled his drinks and waited for the men to go back to the governor's house. Even at this distance and this late date, Harpe's bloody deeds were known to enough men, like Roger himself, to insure swift retribution. In that case, Roger's task was finished.

The men came up the street again, and Roger marveled that Setton had the courage to walk back into the lion's den. It was as Stump had suggested, you never could tell about Harpe. At times he was shrewd, at other times he wasn't. He seemed to get something in his head and he would do some extremely idiotic things to carry it out. There was no explaining him because you never knew whether he was going to be reasonable or foolhardy—and in that fashion he had gotten by for a long time. It began to look, thought Roger, as if his time was about to come to an end. If it came to an end on a gallows at Natchez, that was as good as the bough of an oak tree farther up the Trace. Roger put down his glass and followed the crowd.

The butler opened the door and said to Setton and May, "Will you two gen'lemen step inside, suh? The gov'nor will see you in a minute."

Setton must have sensed something wrong, for he glanced at May. May looked questioning. Setton looked back at the crowd and then seemed to make up his mind. Perhaps he reasoned that he had to go through with it or face the crowd. He motioned to May, and they stepped in.

A moment later they were coming out again, each with a pistol in his back. The big-bellied sheriff was holding the one at Setton's back, a deputy was holding the one at May's back. "I'll hold you both until we see if anybody can identify you," the sheriff said. "If you're Little Harpe, you'll hang from the neck. That I'll vouch for."

"Little Harpe!" somebody breathed. "Is that Little Harpe from Kentucky?"

"If it is," growled another man, "I want the privilege of cutting his throat myself."

"Like hell!" another exclaimed. "The Harpes killed my brother!"

"Let's take care of him now!"

"Everybody cool off," the sheriff said. "He's in the hands of the law."

"Maybe you'll let him go back across the river."

"We're not lettin' him go nowhere," the sheriff said, "until we find out for damn' sure who he is. Now move back."

Roger looked at the terrible scowl on Setton's face, and drew a deep breath. The tables had turned suddenly but completely.

That night small printed posters appeared in the saloons along the river:

237

Notice! It is believed that WILEY HARPE, commonly known as LITTLE HARPE, or RED-HEADED HARPE, has been captured. If any Kentucky boatman has any personal knowledge of Harpe, let him come to the jail and see if he can identify him.

Sheriff of the Circuit Court.
Fredk. Fleshman

There was speculation and excitement along the shelf that night, and much talk of violence. A few men quietly got into their boats and set off down the river. But there were five who gathered in the Boatmen's Bar who swore they would know Little Harpe if they met him face to face. One said he had been with a companion whom the Harpes had killed. Others had encountered them at various places in Kentucky.

Roger, saying nothing, followed the five to the jail the next morning. They sat in the sheriff's office chewing and spitting while the sheriff brought Setton, sullen-faced, out to be inspected. Setton's tomahawk was on the table.

Two of the men said right off, "That's Little Harpe, all right." A third walked all the way around him and then looked into the unpleasant face and said, "That's Wiley Harpe, as cold-blooded a killer as ever set foot on Kentucky soil!"

The fourth said, "It's been several years since I seen him, and that was after sundown in the forest, but I think it's the same one, all right."

The fifth had been a witness against the Harpes for the killing of Langford. "I knew him well," he said. "He and his brother escaped from jail at Danville before the trial. But I helped the sheriff guard them when they went down to the crick to wash. The sheriff let them take off their clothes." He stared at Setton. "I remember two marks on Little Harpe. He had a big mole low on his neck, and his second and third toes was growed together."

Harpe scowled. "You're trying to make me out somebody I never was. You don't want to see me collect the reward money."

"I don't give a damn about that. Mason is well rid of, and no regrets. But if you're Little Harpe you're a worse murderer than Mason."

The sheriff was behind Setton. He seized the collar of his hunting shirt and turned it down. A big mole showed brown against the white skin. Setton jerked away from him. "You've got no right to do that."

"You're a prisoner," the sheriff reminded him. "We got all kinds of rights with a prisoner."

"I'm not Harpe! I told you, I'm John Setton."

"You're John Taylor too, aren't you?"

"Yes, I've been called John Taylor."

"How about Wells?" asked the sheriff.

Harpe's eyes were furious. "They have called me Wells—but I am not Harpe. I was with Mason at Little Prairie, and he said there my name was Setton."

"We could hold you for the murder of Mason—if that was Mason's head."

Harpe swung on him. "The governor said dead or alive."

The sheriff sat on the edge of the table. "Take off your shoes and let's see them toes."

Setton growled, "Lots of men have toes growed together."

One of the five boatmen spoke up, dubiously now, "It might be, sheriff. Sometimes men look an almighty lot alike when they ain't the same men. I don't know if I'm sure about this feller or not."

"Well," said the one who had been at Danville, "that might be right—but this feller sure resembles him."

The sheriff was disgusted. "How am I going to get a conviction when you ain't even sure?"

"What's the matter with Stump?" asked the man from Danville.

The sheriff stared at him. "He ain't sure either."

"I tell you I'm not Harpe," said Setton. "I never saw the man in my life."

"Where did you meet up with Mason?"

"I come up from New Orleans and ran into Mason."

"Where is May from?" the sheriff asked suddenly.

"He ain't never told and I never ast. I met up with him at the Boatmen's Bar."

"And you robbed a man near Hunston."

"We never killed anybody."

"But you are an outlaw?"

"We robbed once in a while when we needed money. That's all. We never killed nobody. And I ain't Harpe. I never been in Kentucky Country in my life. I don't know nothin' about Danville or any jail."

The sheriff looked confused.

"I'm tellin' the honest-to-God truth," said Setton. "I never been near Kentucky except when I was with Mason at Little Prairie. It ain't fair to arrest me for something I don't know anything about."

The sheriff was uncomfortable. He looked at Setton and at those who had identified him. "You wouldn't want to be the cause of hangin' an innocent man, would you?" he asked.

Heads shook slowly.

"Well, then, if you ain't Harpe—"

"Wait a minute," said Roger, and pushed forward.

Setton turned to scowl at him, and the man's eyes were maniacal with sudden fury.

"What's on your mind, mister?" asked the sheriff.

"I can identify this man for you," said Roger.

The sheriff hesitated. He looked at Setton and then at Roger. "Who are you?"

"Roger Adams, from up on the Trace. I know this man. I knew him from Knoxville."

Setton said hoarsely, "His word is no good. He's a deserter. He deserted from the army!"

Roger half smiled. "You see, he knows me, sheriff. He has convicted himself."

The sheriff nodded, his big head making exaggerated movements. "Sounds like somethin' to me," he said. "He sure admitted knowing you—but how can identify him?"

Roger took a deep breath. To a certain extent this

was a bluff, and as a rule he wasn't much of a bluffer. "If he's Little Harpe," he said, "he will have a small scar under his left nipple."

He saw the hate shine in Setton's eyes, and knew the gamble had paid off. "I've already showed you my neck and took off my shoes!" Harpe shouted. "How far does the law require me to go. This ain't no court!"

Roger saw the sheriff again undecided, and it seemed to him the sheriff was doing a lot of leaning over backward. Roger took a quick step forward, grasped Setton's shirt, one side in each hand, and ripped it open, his eyes fixed on Setton's left side. A small diagonal scar showed against the dead white skin.

Harpe spun. He lifted his tomahawk from the table and snatched the sheriff's pistol from his belt. The sheriff stumbled and fell sidewise, and left Roger facing Harpe. Harpe took a quick step forward, shoved the pistol into Roger's stomach, and pulled the trigger. It snapped.

Roger's long arms were coming up. Harpe threw the pistol underhanded at his face. He felt the sight tear a furrow through his cheek. Then he closed with Harpe and tried to avoid the tomahawk.

Harpe chopped at him with the blade, viciously, at his face, at his head. Blood poured over one eye from a cut in his scalp, but he got one hand on Harpe's right wrist and pushed it high and to the man's rear. They were in a corner, with Roger's body shielding Harpe's, and the men stood around, watching. May must have started to move, for Roger heard somebody grunt, "Stay out of this fight, mister. You might get hurt!"

The sheriff was getting to his feet, but offered no interference. This was a frontier fight, and as such was above even the law. Roger had now to subdue Harpe, and he wanted to do it without killing him, for he wanted the law to take its course with the man.

On the ridge, a lonely place in the winter, was the body of Jeff, a young boy who had somehow gone wrong but who had been encouraged by Wiley Harpe. The law had taken its way with Jeff. The law should take its way with Harpe.

He pinned the man against the logs but he could not break his grip on the tomahawk. It was like trying to hold a squirming cat. The man got away from him, got room to swing the hatchet. Roger stepped inside the swing and got both hands on Harpe's right wrist. He bent the arm back and down, behind Harpe's head until the tomahawk clattered on the floor.

A sudden intake of breath from the spectators warned him of a new danger, and he twisted, to see Harpe pulling his own tomahawk out of its loop with his left hand.

He sliced off a piece of scalp as big as a peso, before Roger finally got him down. His blood was dripping on Harpe's face, and Harpe's teeth bared like an animal's as he tried to get up. But Roger held him down at the biceps of each arm. Harpe raised his head to sink his teeth into Roger's shoulder, but Roger butted him in the face until the man finally went limp.

Roger looked up, found the sheriff with his one unobscured eye. "He's your man, sheriff. This is Little Harpe. Do you want him or do you want me to take care of him for you?"

The sheriff had his pistol back. "I reckon I'll take him now. I'm obliged to you, mister."

Roger stayed on in Natchez, grimly determined to see Harpe to the end. By now the identification convinced the most skeptical, for more rivermen had come forward, identifying him in many different ways.

"They's only one way for 'em to get out of it now," said the bartender at the Boatmen's Bar.

"How is that?" asked Roger.

"They got to escape."

Roger studied his drink. "You think they will?"

"Wouldn't you?"

Roger said, "I think I'll go up on the hill."

In a few days the bartender's prediction was substantiated. The sheriff, looking incredulous, kept pointing to the side of the log cabin that served as a jail. "They whittled all the way through a log," he said, "and pushed it loose. I never figgered on anything like that."

"They whittled?" asked Roger. "Where did they get knives?"

The sheriff shook his head. He couldn't understand it.

Roger loaded up his wallet, got the chestnut, and started out on their trail. He found them near Hunston, roasting a wild turkey on a spit over a smoky fire in a persimmon grove. He crawled to the edge of the brush that surrounded the grove, cautiously poked his rifle through, and said, "Surrender, Harpe, or I'll blow your head off."

Roger had been ready for a gunshot, sudden flight, or a flying tomahawk, but Harpe, caught unaware, did not seem to be able to think. He looked at Roger, then raised his hands slowly over his head.

Roger ordered May to lie down on his face. Roger picked out Harpe's tomahawk and his knife. He turned his face to a persimmon tree and tied him there, while Harpe, seemingly numb at this sudden change of fortune, offered no resistance.

Roger got them tied to his liking, put them on their blaze-faced horses and tied the rear horse's bridle to the lead horse's saddle so that if they ran away they would have to run together. This way he took them to Hunston and turned them over to the sheriff there.

Then he settled down to watch. For a long time he had waited for justice. He had seen him identified and then allowed to escape. Now he had brought them back once more, and he would still have to see it through, although he had been away from Anne and home for months, and it was not a thing he could forget.

On January 13, 1804, he heard the grand jury bring an indictment of robbery against each of them. He listened intently to two weeks of legal sparring—for now the two men were represented by high-priced legal counsel from Natchez—and then they went on trial. Elisha Winters, who lived up near New Madrid, had heard of their arrest at Natchez and had come down to testify against them. He was now brought up to Hunston for the two trials. Both men were found guilty, and on February fourth Roger was in the court-room when the three judges called Wiley Harpe before them. Those in the room stood up while Judge Thomas Rodney pronounced the sentence.

"John Setton, you have been found guilty of robbery of one Elisha Winters. It is the sentence of this court that on Wednesday, February eighth, 1804, you be taken to the place of execution and there hung up by the neck, between the hours of ten o'clock in the forenoon and four o'clock in the afternoon, until you are dead, dead, dead. The sheriff of Jefferson County is hereby ordered to carry out this sentence."

Roger took a deep breath, while Little Harpe, the murderer, stood there, his face locked in that scowl that was his trademark, his hair low on his forehead, his eyes smoldering with hate. But finally, against the force and majesty of the law, even Little Harpe's murderous reputation failed to strike terror.

Roger was there also when, about three o'clock in the afternoon, the sheriff led the two men on foot to the gallows field a little way north of Hunston, followed by at least a hundred and fifty spectators, some of them women and children, most of them seeming to feel a festive spirit in the occasion.

It was a long walk in the bright winter sun, but, like

all walks, it came to an end. A heavy pole had been placed high between two trees, and from the pole dropped two ropes.

Roger thought of the oak bough from which they had hung Jeff. For whatever part Little Harpe had had in steering Jeff down the wrong path, he was about to pay. Frontier justice was crude, and sometimes it was slow, but eventually the laws of society caught up even with a man like Little Harpe.

Each man's hands were tied behind him. Two men held a ladder under one rope, and the sheriff said to May, "Climb."

May tried to protest, but the sheriff pushed him toward the ladder. Two more men held the ladder while the sheriff went up after him. He caught the end of the rope and tied it around May's neck. Then he tied May's feet together and got down. The men continued to hold the ladder in place.

The sheriff spun Wiley Harpe toward a second ladder. He likewise got the rope around his neck, and his two feet were tied together.

The sheriff got back on the ground and stood off a little way. "John Setton," he said, "or Wiley Harpe, whichever you be, have you anything to say?"

Harpe scowled. His ugly face was an incarnation of evil. He stared at the sheriff, looked around him, met Roger's eyes but did not seem to recognize him, and looked back at the sheriff.

Roger was puzzled for a moment. Then he saw that Harpe's hate for him had not been a personal animosity but a hate of all mankind. Roger as an individual meant nothing to him. And Roger saw too, in that brief moment, that his own feeling against Harpe was not as much a personal thing as it was a determination that outlaws should not rule the Trace.

"John May, you got anything to say?"

"I have! I haven't done anything to be hung for!" May stretched his neck to get away from the scratchiness of the rope. "I did the Territory a good turn by getting rid of old Mason, and you reward me by—"

The sheriff's arm dropped. In unison the eight men backed away from the ladders and let them fall. Harpe and May swung high, struggling for a few minutes. Both of their faces turned blue. Presently they quit struggling.

"Take 'em down now, sheriff?"

"No, leave 'em up a while. The court order says they must be dead."

Roger relaxed. Even in death Little Harpe looked mean, and, seeing him swing there, Roger had half expected something to happen to save him. But now there was no doubt. The sheriff said to leave them there for a while; he was taking no chances.

The crowd waited, watching the bodies sway in the wind. Finally the sheriff gave the word, "Cut them down."

"Untie the knot," said somebody, "and save the rope."

The sheriff looked at two buzzards far overhead. "Any way—just get 'em down."

Roger watched the corpse of Wiley Harpe. It was hardly on the ground before a man stepped up and listened for his heartbeat. He got up and shook his head. "He's dead."

"I heerd your knees crack, doc."

"That wasn't my knees. It was your head rattling."

A woman laughed, high, shrilly. A man stepped up to Harpe with a knife in his hand. "He's dead for sure, doc?"

The physician nodded. The man stooped and began to cut. Somebody helped him from the other side. The bones in Little Harpe's neck crunched as his head was twisted off exactly as his brother's had been over five years before. Roger turned away. There was no longer any question about Wiley Harpe.

They cut off May's head, and set one of the heads on a pole alongside the trail. They took the other one west of Hunston and set it up also on the trail. "Just so nobody gets any ideas," the decapitator said. "This here territory is law-abidin' from here on. If anybody's got any different ideas, let 'em take a look at them two heads."

"What you gonna do with the bodies, Sheriff?"

"Bury them in the graveyard."

"The buzzards'll do a better job and do it cheaper."

"You've got their heads. What are you squawking about?"

"I got kin buried in that graveyard. I don't want them two carcasses there."

But late that night the two bodies were put into one box and buried alongside the Trace, almost under one of the heads.

Roger Adams had a last drink and went to bed heavily. He had one more job to do. It wouldn't be easy, but he was going to do it anyway.

18 THE NEXT MORNING before sunup Roger had his journey cakes and bacon and a cup of coffee. He saddled the chestnut and rode north, past the scowling head of Wiley Harpe, on up the Trace, back toward home.

He met John Swaney three days out—Swaney with his half bushel of shelled corn in a towsack and his tin horn and his wallet fat with mail. "Lots of mail coming down the Trace now," said Swaney. "We took over Louisiana in December, you know."

"Heard about it." Roger was preoccupied.

"Lots of people coming down the Trace too. The country's settling up. Your territory will be part of Mississippi before long, they say. Make you feel pretty good, I reckon, to have law and order after being out there by yourself so long."

Roger nodded slowly. Law and order—with him a deserter whose word had no legal standing, who was even subject to court-martial. Law and order meant that after all these years those things were catching up with him. Hughes had known. Hughes had died. But Hughes had told Harpe, and now Harpe was dead. But always there would be others. Somebody would come along who would know—and what then?

This was the problem that Roger had to work out. And there was not much time left.

Swaney, chewing on a piece of jerked beef, said, "You heard about the new land law?"

"Can't say I have?"

"Special pre-emption act. All squatters south of Tennessee and north of Mississippi Territory can buy six hundred forty acres at two dollars an acre if they can prove they were living on the land in 1795. I guess that counts you in, doesn't it?"

"I guess it does." That was one burden off of his mind, anyway. There never had been any question that squatters in his neighborhood had come to that land illegally, but most of them had gotten along with the Indians and had minded their own business, and after a while the Indians had accepted them. It was still technically illegal, but nobody had worried, for the same thing had happened a hundred times: whites moved in, the government made a treaty with the Indians and gave the whites a chance to settle the title to their land.

"All you have to do," said Swaney, "is prove your citizenship and pay down a fourth. How much land you got there, Adams?"

"Close to five hundred acres cleared."

"Cost you two hundred and fifty dollars a year. Well, you're sittin' high in the saddle. Just keep a sharp watch for speculators. Understand there'll be a land office opened in your neighborhood, come spring."

Land office. Two dollars an acre. Prove citizenship. Finally he asked Swaney, "You see my family?"

"Sure. All fine. You got two new blacks and a new grandchild."

Roger looked up. "Liz?"

"Sure."

The next question was a hard one, for it was not the kind a man on the frontier generally asked:

"Is Anne—all right?"

"Fine, Roger. Better looking every day. You better get home before I take a notion to stop overnight at your place." He laughed boisterously and slapped Roger on the back. "Best lookin' wife in the Territory, and he stays away for months. Why, Roger? There's no Indians to fight any more."

"There are white outlaws worse than any Indians— and there is always oneself."

Swaney shook his head. "Gotta be movin'. Dispatches from Washin'ton in this bunch."

Roger watched him jog off down the Trace. Then he swung into the saddle and went on north.

It was now approaching the middle of February. With a wide-open port at New Orleans, the river would soon be swarming with flatboats and the Trace would be traveled hourly by people going southwest. Lots of those travelers would stop here and there to take up land. Some might have been with Morgan.

As people settled down and danger receded, they began to ask questions about their neighbors. There would be questions about his own past. Where had he come from? When had he settled on the Trace? Where had he fought during the war? What battles had he been in?

He drew off the trail that night and camped in a

grove of sugar maples, and smoked his cob pipe thoughtfully after a meal of parched corn. Up on the Trace now they would be rolling logs, mauling rails, burning brush, getting ready to plow. On his own place, Anne would see that things were going. Anne knew as well as any man what had to be done.

He was thinking of Anne as he wrapped his blanket around him and raked up a pile of leaves as a pillow. Anne had come to the Trace with him the day after they had been married; she had worked hard and never complained; she had borne his children and raised them; she had grandchildren nine miles below them on the Trace. It would be cruel to uproot Anne, abandon their home, and move on west.

Twenty years before, the Trace had seemed so far west that he hadn't really considered that a time might come when he would be crowded, or, if he had, that time had seemed to be far in the future—too far to worry about. Now suddenly that time was here. The twenty years were gone. They had been a long and eventful twenty years, but the memory of their riding horseback down the Trace, of his saying, "This ought to make good land. There's water close by, and plenty of woods," and Anne's saying, "We could build our cabin right there on the little knoll"—all those were as if they had happened yesterday. And already the indefinite and distant future had become now.

He rode on north in the morning, and the next day he saw that the better places were being taken up by new settlers. In the early afternoon he passed the turn-off to Nicholson's, and later he could see smoke rising from the chimney of Coates' place. Then he noted with approval that his son-in-law had cleared off twenty acres more during the winter. He saw no one about, but there were sounds of activity beyond the cabin, and he guessed they were clearing the briars out of the land opened up the year before.

The hum of the spinning wheel was loud as he rode into his own yard. His three children stared at him as if he were a stranger—which, in a way, he was. Will was fifteen—almost a man. He came up from the cane with a grubbing hoe on his shoulder.

Roger took the chestnut to the pen. Gene took charge of it. "He looks right peart, Mist' Adams. Been feedin' good down on the Trace."

"Pretty well."

Gene's eyes rolled. "That Natchez town, they say she's the wickedest town in the United States."

"Natchez won't last long," Roger said absently. "Law is coming in everywhere."

He went to the door of the big cabin and pulled the latchstring, pushed the door. Anne turned from the spinning wheel, one hand manipulating the small, fluffy roll of wool. He set his rifle in the corner and hung his powder horn on a peg. When he turned around she said, her eyes large, "I'll make coffee, Rog."

She started around the spinning wheel and brushed against him, and suddenly he was holding her, strong and willowy. "It's been so long, Rog!" she whispered.

"Yes." He held her for a moment and then let her go, and now she was hardly able to keep her eyes from him.

Betty, now thirteen, and Sarah, eleven, came in and ranged themselves along the wall. He looked at them and smiled, and they went back.

He watched Anne stirring the fire to heat water in the kettle, and for the first time since he could remember, her movements were inept and aimless, as they had been the first night they had been by themselves, and abruptly he felt very tender toward her, and knew it would be an incredibly cruel thing to tear her from this home they had made in the wilderness. Yet if the land commissioner found him, a deserter, squatting on land that belonged to the United States, what could he do but order them to move on?

That night for supper they had wild pigeons with wheat bread dumplings and ash cake, honey for sweetening, dried apples for sauce.

Roger looked around the cabin. He got up and put his rifle on the antlers over the fireplace. He straightened the bearskin rug, saw that the big salt gourd was in place, along with the powder gourd. Hanging by the fireplace was a smaller salt gourd with a finger hole at one side for breaking loose the salt when it became caked from wet weather. The meal gum or log section, hollowed out to store meal and with a top on to serve also as a stool, stood by the fire. Strings of dried pumpkin hung from the roof. He pushed the ends of the log into the center of the fire, and sat down.

After supper the girls went out to play and Will followed. Anne sat down to work at the wheel. Roger moved about restlessly, until finally she said, "Something on your mind, Rog?"

"Maybe."

"What about Little Harpe?"

"His head is stuck up on a pole alongside the Trace." She shuddered. "The Harpes came to a bad end."

"It was an end that suited them. They lived violent, murderous lives."

"What part did you play?"

"I kept track of him to be sure he didn't get away, and I identified him at the last, when he was claiming to be somebody else."

She picked up another small roll of wool from the pile on the floor, and deftly threaded it into the one nearly gone. "I've never seen you so nervous. Are you afraid of his gang?"

"Harpe didn't really have any gang. Mason did, but Mason's dead too. No, I don't think there'll ever be anybody try to get revenge for Wiley Harpe."

"Then you ought to be ready to quiet down, after four months' being gone." She glanced at him sidewise. "It'll soon be bedtime, Rog."

He looked at her, took a long breath, and closed his eyes. His words were peevish. "Anne, you're the only woman I've wanted for twenty years—but I've got something else on my mind now—something that's got to be settled." He paused. "I hope you understand."

She glanced up at him and then back at her work.

The hum of the wheel was loud and continuous. "It isn't like you," she said, "but I'll try."

He touched her shoulder gently. Then he went to the horse pen and saddled the chestnut. He rode out of the yard at a fast trot. He heard the children playing Crack the Whip with the Negro children in the woods next to the stubblefield, and it reminded him he must get out there tomorrow and take a look at the new deadening, to see if it was safe to walk under. Then he turned the chestnut down the Trace.

A little over an hour later he passed Coates' place, and saw the yellow light of a candle through the brush. He'd like to see them all, but not now. He went on until he reached the narrow trail that turned off to Hiram Hall's, and followed it through a thick grove to the small clearing where Hall's cabin sat.

He was met by the usual pack of yapping dogs, who stayed just out of range of the chestnut's heels. The door opened and Hall peered into the darkness. "Who's out there?"

"Roger Adams."

Hall stepped down into the yard. "Git, you hounds! Git!" He came closer to Roger and said, "'Light, Adams, 'light."

Roger dismounted. He led the chestnut to one side, and Hall followed.

"Hear you had quite a tussle with outlaws down by Natchez."

"It's all over now."

"Bring back any heads?"

"The heads are on posts alongside the Trace, just to remind anybody who wants to do some outlawing what he can expect from now on in the Territory."

"It was high time," said Hall. "You did a good piece of work for us along the Trace."

"That isn't why I'm here," Roger said abruptly.

Hall's answer was slow. "It ain't?"

Roger said, "Do you remember the men on the jury that—found Jeff guilty?"

"Yes, reckon I do, but—"

"I want to meet them tomorrow morning—at the same place."

Hall sounded reluctant. "Looky here, Roger, I hope you ain't going to start somethin' over that."

Roger paid no attention. "The Regulators are still organized, aren't they?"

"Sure."

"Their judgments still go, don't they?"

"Far as I know."

"And there's no other law here, is there?"

"There's rumors of a judge comin' in, but we ain't seen him yet."

"Then," Roger said fiercely, "I want to put a man on trial tomorrow."

"Anybody we know?"

"Yes," Roger said. "Me."

"You!" Hall sucked in his breath. "Whatta you been up to?"

"You'll find out tomorrow morning." Roger got into the saddle and rode the chestnut out of the yard.

He reached home at midnight and went to the whisky keg. He got a cup of rye—quietly, so as not to awaken even Anne—filled his cob pipe with tobacco from the fragrant barrel, and went out in the yard to sit on a stump and watch the moon rise through the tall, straight persimmon trees that, like overgrown saplings, had no branches until near the top.

He heard a movement, and turned. Anne, in her night dress, said, "Move over a little, Rog, and I'll watch it with you."

He moved over, and she sat down. He put his arm around her. It was February. She shivered a little and leaned closer against him.

He took his pipe out of his mouth. "Always liked that moon coming up through the persimmons," he said. "It always seemed kind of like our trademark."

She nodded. "It's our land. It'll always be our land now."

He didn't answer. Presently he arose and picked her up in his arms and carried her into the house. . . .

At breakfast the next morning he said to Anne, "You better go with me today."

She looked at him, not understanding but not questioning. There never would be another like Anne.

They rode down the trail to Coates' and turned off. They went across the field, and Anne drew back in surprise. "Men there! It's—like a jury!"

"It is a jury," Roger said harshly. "You're going to know all about me, Anne."

"Roger! You weren't—an outlaw?"

"No," he said soberly. "You'll hear it all pretty soon."

She stayed by him, riding sidesaddle. He reached the big oak tree and looked at the men under it. "Are they all here?" he asked Hiram Hall.

"All but Hickory Wade. He's got the chills."

"Have you got somebody to take his place?"

"This is a democratic country. I reckon the jury can pick another man."

The eleven men conferred. Finally Kuykendall spoke up. "We'll take Jim Porter, yer honor."

"All right. Jim, you git over there with the jury."

A short, pot-bellied man in moccasins went to take his place.

"Now, then, Roger Adams, I reckon we're set up for business."

Roger got to his feet. He was taller than most of these men, and younger, for he was still under forty. He looked at them all and turned to Hall and said, "Your honor, I want to be tried by the same court that tried my son. I have no more right to expect mercy than he did."

He heard sharp intakes of breath. Anne was sitting on the ground.

"What's the charge?" asked Hall.

"Desertion from the Army of the United States."

Hall squinted at him. "You ain't old enough."

"I'm old enough."

Anne was watching him intently. He could detect no emotion on her face except disbelief.

"Prob'ly you better tell us about it," said Hall.

"I'll do that. My father was a rich merchant in London. He got me into Tarleton's Dragoons, and I came to this country to fight on the side of the British."

Hall's eyes were narrow. "You was with Tarleton in Carolina?"

"Yes."

"I got this wooden leg from Tarleton," said Bill Crowley. "He'da let me rot."

Roger said, "I know. It didn't take long to find out what Tarleton was like, and I deserted from the British Army about two weeks before the battle of Cowpens."

"That's no crime," said Hall. "Anybody who deserted from Tarleton deserves a medal."

"That isn't the whole story. I disappeared in the woods. Both sides had spies everywhere, and in about a week I located General Morgan's headquarters."

"Dan Morgan?" asked Hall.

"Yes."

"I served under Dan Morgan myself."

"I intended to," said Roger. "I found a man scalped by the Indians, and I took his clothes and left my British uniform and went to Morgan's headquarters. I told them I had been fighting Indians along the Ohio, and that I wanted to join up to fight the British."

"Best move you ever made," said Crowley.

"I liked Morgan. He handled his men well, and he was humane, and he was fighting a tough war against an old campaigner. Tarleton was no fool."

"I can vouch for that!" exclaimed Jim Porter.

"They heard my story and accepted it. They swore me into the Army of the United States, and General Morgan put me on his staff because I could read and write."

"Then you deserted Morgan?" asked Hall, somewhat grimly.

"Yes. One night by candlelight I was writing out dispatches for Morgan's officers when a man—obviously a spy—came into Morgan's tent. I had seen him before, for he had pretended to be a spy for Tarleton. I didn't know whose side he was really on, and I was scared. I saw that he recognized me, and I was afraid he would tell Morgan that I had been with Tarleton—and Morgan would have had me shot as a spy. So I kept on with my work while this man watched me, making his report to Morgan. It sounded to me as if he was on the side of the rebels, and I knew that if he was he would turn me in to Morgan. Once that happened, I wouldn't have a chance—so I folded the paper I was working on, went to the door of the tent, stepped outside, and went into the forest. I never went back."

"How old was you when this happened?" asked Hall.

"Seventeen."

"What did you do then—go back to the British?"

"No. I went farther west and joined up with some long hunters against the Indians. The war ended soon after that, and when we heard the news I was staying near Louisville. My wife's father had made a station there, and after the war was over we got married and came down here on the Trace.

"So you're really a double deserter."

"Yes."

"You ever fight against the Americans again?"

"Not to my knowledge."

"Why are you telling us this?" asked Hall. "Nobody was botherin' you, was they?"

"Nobody but me."

Hall looked at him. "What was the man's name who was spyin' for Morgan—the man you was afraid of?"

"Tarleton knew him as Samuelson. I never heard what Morgan called him."

"Do you know if he turned you in?"

"No."

"You ever see anybody from Morgan's outfit after you came West?"

"Nobody but this man who had been a spy."

"Where is he now?"

"He is dead. He was killed up north of Nashville a while back."

"I want to know somethin'," said Hall. "Why are you testifyin' agin yourself? The army ain't going to come down here after twenty years, lookin' for a man who served one week."

"Probably not," said Roger. "But a man has to live with his conscience. He has to pay for these things sometime or his wife and children will have to pay."

"How do you figger?"

Roger looked at Anne, hoping she would understand. "This man Samuelson—or Hughes, as he called himself when he came to Kentutcky—told Wiley Harpe about me, and Harpe knew. That's one reason Harpe came up here on the Trace and got Jeff in with him. He figured he could hold that over me and I would have to protect him."

"That why you went to Natchez after him?"

"Yes."

"You got him, didn't you?"

"Yes. The law hanged him."

"Well, them two are dead, and as far as you know they are the only ones who knew about you. Why not let a sleeping dog lie?"

"That's what I was doing when Harpe started working along the Trace here—and you see what happened."

Hall looked at the oak bough over his head. "But that's all over. He's dead and he can't bother you no more."

Roger shook his head decisively. "I've done this thing. I've been a deserter. I want to get it out in the open so it can't come up to throw a shadow over my wife and my children. It might be that if I had done this before, that Jeff—"

"I don't go along with you there," said Hall. "What's going to happen is going to happen. If it wasn't Harpe it would be somebody else. But I think I get your point, all right. If you got something coming you want to get it over with."

"That's right."

"When did you settle on the Trace?"

"In 1784."

"Was you the first one down here?"

"I was the first one in this section."

Kuykendall spoke up. "I got a question, Mr. Adams, You said your pa was a rich man."

"Yes."

"I take it he had consid'able property."

"I believe so."

"You ever tried to get in line for any of that property?"

"Of course not. I gave that up when I left Tarleton."

"Your pa still alive?"

"I don't know," said Roger. "I've never had any communication with them from that time."

"If there ain't no more questions," said Hiram Hall, "you and the missus go down to visit with Liz while we decide what to do with this here case."

"All right."

They went across the field. Liz opened the door and chased away the dogs, and they went in. Liz said, "I was making some dittany tea."

"It would taste good,' said Anne.

"What's it this time—a boy or a girl?" asked Roger.

"A boy. We called him Roger."

Roger smiled. He felt free and easy for the first time in years.

Liz poured boiling water in a pot and looked anxiously at Roger. "The men up on the hill—under the oak tree—"

"Regulators," said Roger.

Anne said quietly, "I am very proud of your father."

He turned to her and saw her break into tears. He looked at Liz. She had developed into a tall girl with nice breasts and hips like her mother's. Now that he noticed, she was getting to be a good-looking girl, too.

Anne drank her tea and said nervously, "They're taking a long time up there."

Roger said soberly, "It's a serious offense."

He roamed about the cabin. It was strong, well-built. The chinking was still tight. The gourds were filled with salt and honey and gunpowder. "It's nice to see you doing well," he said.

Liz nodded. "We're doing fine." But he saw that she was worried.

Then Coates halloed from across the field. Roger got up. "You stay," he said to Anne. "I'll be back in a little while."

"I'm going," she said. "Whatever it is, I've got to know."

They went across the field, down one row a few steps and then across it to the next one.

Coates was walking back toward the oak tree. Roger looked at the emotionless faces of the jury, and abruptly he was scared. Desertion was a serious crime. A deserter could be executed. He had put his life into the hands of these twelve men.

He walked up the slope soberly, and it seemed that it was cold where the trees threw a shadow across his way.

Hiram Hall cleared his throat, seeming a little embarrassed, and Roger braced himself.

"Lem Kuykendall, you're foreman of the jury. What does the jury find?"

Kuykendall stood up. He spit tobacco juice at the foot of the tree. Then he faced Roger.

"The jury finds you guilty of desertion, Roger Adams. It also finds that you have been on the Trace for twenty years and have been a good citizen, so we recommended that sentence be suspended."

"Oh!" said Anne.

Roger smiled. He went up to shake their hands. Hall was the last one. He said, "Your neighbors already forgot about this, Roger, but in case some high-flyin' judge comes along, remember you already been tried once, and they can't try you twice for the same thing."

Roger stared at him. "Where'd you learn stuff like that?"

"Back in New Jersey," Hall said. "I had a job cleaning floors in the courthouse." He squinted at the sun. "Well, gotta be goin'. If I'da stayed on that job long enough I mighta learned to read even."

Roger and Anne went by Coates' place. Coates was out at the trial to shake hands. "You sure had me sweatin'," he said. "They could of done all kinds of things to you."

"They didn't," said Roger. "And I'll never have to worry about it any more. I'm glad I got it out of my system."

He and Anne rode up the Trace. "Some day," he said, "The Trace will be wide enough for vehicles.

There'll be a regular wagon road from Nashville to Natchez."

Anne turned to him, her brown eyes and weathered face intent under her sundown. "Let them come," she said, "and let them go. The Trace is our home. Here we'll stay."

He nodded. He saw the tears in her eyes and pressed her forearm with his strong fingers. "Here we'll stay," he said softly.

Center Point Publishing

600 Brooks Road ● PO Box 1
Thorndike ME 04986-0001 USA

(207) 568-3717

US & Canada:
1 800 929-9108
www.centerpointlargeprint.com